Best Summer Vacation Ever

Anthony Lombardi

Copyright © 2023 Anthony Lombardi

All rights reserved. No part of this book may be reproduced or transmitted in any form or by any means, electronic or mechanical, including photocopying, recording or by any information storage and retrieval system without permission in writing from the publisher.

Mitt Madd Publishing—Murfreesboro, TN
ISBN: 979-8-218-30872-8
Library of Congress Control Number: 2023923971
Title: *Best Summer Vacation Ever!*
Author: Anthony Lombardi
Digital distribution | 2023
Paperback | 2023

Dedication

I would like to thank the three most important women in my life. My mom who always gave me words of encouragement and unconditional love. My sister for always being there to support me and most importantly to my wife who is my puzzle piece and the source of every inspiration I have.

To my incredible children, Dog boy and Sweet P, I love you so much and I am thankful every day I get to see and give you hugs.

To my brothers, sister and cousins who helped inspire the book.

To the IHOP restaurant in Murfreesboro, TN for allowing me to spend countless hours at my booth writing the book and to all the servers who made sure I never ran out of Iced-tea.

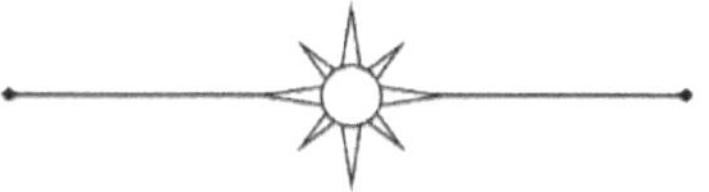

Summer Vacation

It was the summer of 1982. Michael Jackson dominated the air waves, ET was on every movie screen and MTV was the only thing teenagers watched on TV. I just finished my 7th grade year and was getting ready to rule middle school as the ultimate upper classmen. But before I started my journey in the big time my family decided to have the ultimate family vacation.

My mom and dad wanted to have a semi-family reunion slash vacation with my Aunty Louise, my mom's sister and my Uncle John, who was my dad's brother. They thought that since my oldest brother Lee and cousin Bill had graduated it would be a great time for all of us to get together. They chose to go to the Clear Lake Family Resort and each family would rent their own home.

All three families headed to the Clear Lake Family Resort the week after school let out for the summer. All the families came from different directions. Aunty Louise lived only 1 and half hours away so they were the first to arrive. We came 3 hours from the South and Uncle John's family had the longest distance so it took them 5 hours from the North.

When our parents first told us about the vacation we all couldn't wait to get together. It was a really cool idea because we all loved hanging with our cousins anytime we could. So here we are for the first time all of us together and we all get to be neighbors for the next 6 weeks. We just knew that this was going to be one of the best summer vacations every. With 10 teenagers ranging between the ages of 13 – 18, what possibly could go wrong?

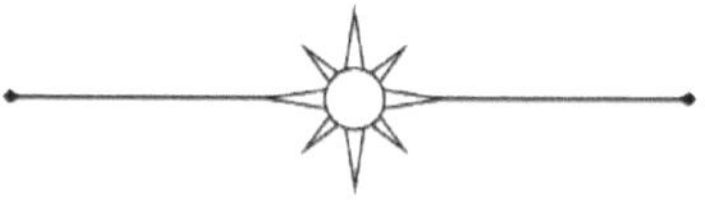

CHAPTER 1
The Families

Aunty Louise Family

Aunty Louise lived about 2 hours from us so we got to see them several times a year. Anytime we visited each other we had great times. Aunty Louise had 3 sons who were all about the same age as my brothers Lee and Richard. Ronald was 16, Raymond was 17 and Bill was 18. Ronald was similar to Richard, not just in age but in mentality. I'll speak more on that later. Raymond was the "go along" guy but Bill on the other hand was just like my brother Lee. He would find ways to come up with things for his younger brothers to do. So naturally he and Lee meshed together really good. Because they had the shortest distance to get to the resort they had arrived before everyone else. Their house was about the same size as ours but was located on the other side of main pool, but what was cool is we could still see their house from our deck.

Uncle John's Family

My Uncle John had 2 children, Sonya who was my sister's age and Johnny who was my age. They were the last family to arrive. They had the smallest house, because I guess Uncle John was the cheapest of all the families. He was one of the Uncles that for your birthday instead of sending you a birthday card filled with money, he'd send a toothbrush in envelop with a handwritten Happy Birthday note. He was too cheap to even splurging on a .50 card Garfield birthday card.

The house he rented only had 1 bedroom and two pullout couch beds in the living room. So instead of having their own bedroom each or even one to share, Sonya and Johnny had to share a pullout couch in the living room. My Uncle owned a plumbing business that was the biggest in his State. So he was like a millionaire but you'd never know it. Probably not even his kids new it. They drove an old two door Yellow AMC Pacer. If you've never seen an AMC Pacer it's like a sardine can with windows all around it. I felt so bad for them because Johnny and Sonya aren't little kids anymore and here they are squished into a backseat of the sardine can. And since they were practically sitting on top of each other, when the climbed out of the car they smelled like sardines also. Whooo Weee did they stink!

When they arrived we all come outside to greet them. Usually we always gave hugs but since they stunk so badly we just gave them air high fives. But at least we did help them with their luggage and get them settled. Although since their "bedroom" was the living room, it was pretty easy to just throw their suitcases in the corner.

After they got settle they took showers to clean up. They must have smelled so bad that we didn't need to tell them they stunk, they instinctively knew their odor was offensive. Well at least Sonya did, which makes sense because she was a girl. Johnny on the other hand, that may have been the only shower he took for the whole 6 week vacation. This guy would give Linus a run for his money in the dirty, smelly category.

We only got to visit with Sonya and Johnny maybe once or twice a year for weekend but every time we got together we always seemed to have fun. Being able to spend 6 weeks was totally awesome because up until this time we never really got a chance to really hang out. So who knew what kind of fun we can have or rather what kind of mischief we could get in to.

My Family

I was the youngest of four children. I was 13 and

my sister Kerry was 15, my brother Richard was 16 and my eldest brother Lee was 18. Lee had just graduated which is one reason my mom thought it would be a great way to celebrate and have a family vacation at the same time. My sister was a great big sister and I'll talk more about that later. She was more of my protector as my older brothers were more of my tormentors.

My older brother Richard was adventurous and somewhat brain dead because some of the stuff he would do was simply crazy. I don't think he ever thought about potential consequences or outcomes of whatever he was about to try. It didn't help that the combination of hormones and marijuana only exacerbated the inability to have a rational thought. Richard's two goals were to find girls and pot. It didn't matter which order but typically getting pot was the main objective for the day for Richard. Pretty much during the early 80's, it seemed like every high school teenager was getting high daily. My brothers and cousins were no different.

Lee was the eldest and he had the best sense of humor. Well, at least he could find a way to laugh at anything. Especially anytime he could talk Richard or his friends to try something crazy. Lee had a way of speaking easy and calmly so just his tone and demeanor would be convincing. He wasn't cruel, he just always thought of ways to have a good time and if someone was dumb enough to try it, then that would make it an even more enjoyable.

My mom was the prototypical mom of the 80's. She was the homemaker but also the CEO of the house. She was the provider, the comforter and the enforcer all wrapped in one. She wanted us be adventurous and encouraged us to get outside, get dirty and even some bumps and bruises. Mom had this saying that if we weren't getting dirty or bruised we weren't playing hard enough. I thought this was cool because as a kid, what better way is there to play.

Dad worked a lot of hours and we usually saw him for dinner and sometimes on the weekends. But we didn't really mind, he was a good dad and we knew he worked hard at his job but also we never went without anything we needed. During our baseball or soccer seasons he would take time to coach our teams or be involved in some way.

Our House

We had the biggest and coolest house at the whole resort. My parents didn't mind splurging from time to time. We had a 5 bedroom "cottage" but it was more like a castle. Mom and dad had their bedroom downstairs and all the kids had bedrooms upstairs. The coolest part of this house is it had a wraparound porch with stairs to walk down to the side yard. We didn't even need to go downstairs to leave the house we could just walk out onto the porch and down the backstairs. It was really cool.

My sister and Sonya clicked right away so Kerry wanted Sonya to stay with her in her room. Since my sister was the only girl in our family, my mom gave up the upstairs master suite. Not only did she have a big room with two beds, she also had her own bathroom. So now at least Sonya didn't have to sleep on a pullout couch in the living room with her stinky brother.

Johnny on the other was a little bit too stinky to stay in my room with me. Besides I had bunk beds and James was already on the top bunk. But on the days when we did go swimming in the lake or pool, we didn't necessarily mind him hanging out with us in our room.

It was pretty cool because all of us kids would be running around from one house to the next…well except for Uncle John's lame house. Nobody really cared about going there, even Johnny and Sonya. From the first time we all got unpacked to the last day we all drove back home, the adventures, mayhem and memories will last us a lifetime.

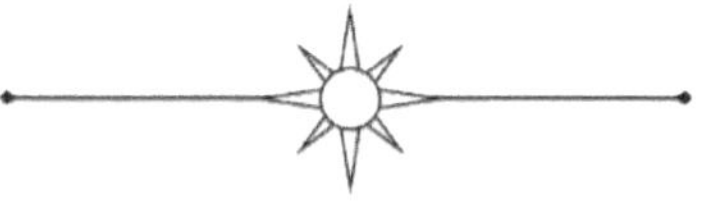

CHAPTER 2

James…my best buddy

My best friend James lived next door to me. He moved next door when we first started Kindergarten and we've been best buddies since. The first time I met him he was playing Matchbox cars in a dirt track he made by the bushes. What 5 year boy doesn't like to play with Matchbox cars? I went inside and grabbed my best numbered race cars and asked mom if I could go next door. During this time, parents were a lot more lenient and let the kids play free in the front yard. It was really cool because both of our lawns joined together so we had like one big front yard to play in.

I ran over to him bringing my bucket of cars and asked if I could play. He was just like me, loved playing in the dirt, getting holes in our jeans and didn't really care if we had snot running out our nose. We just played. It was great in elementary because we always seem to have the same class together. In elementary school we were the coolest kids and everyone wanted to be around us. If we went to the monkey bars, they went to the monkey bars. If we played wall ball, they played wall ball. No matter what we did we were the most popular. Even in class, being the alpha male meant you had the loudest farts. By far, me and James dominated this category and would duke it out in class. All the other kids would laugh and one of us usually got crowned Fart King for the day. It was awesome.

But then we hit middle school and all the rules changed on us. Not to mention our personalities and bodies changed. Now girls that we used to pull hair and push down all the sudden started to look different to us. Especially the ones that started to get boobies in front. For any 7th grade boy, girls that started to look like "real girls" became our focus and we couldn't think about anything else. No more Fart King...girls no longer thought this was cool.

Stephanie and Tiffany were the totally hot girls in 7th grade. We use to play with them all the time just the year earlier but now, something seriously happened to them over the summer. Every day me and James would just talk about them but now that they looked like "real girls," neither one of us had the courage to ever talk to them. Unless you consider throwing paper balls at the back of their heads and then looking around like we didn't know where it came from.

We talked and bragged to the other guys about girls and how cool we were because we knew they all liked us. When the guys would ask, "Why don't you talk to girls?"

We'd say it was because we ignore them by choice. The fact is, if anyone of the girls would have even looked our way, we would probably have peed our pants. That pretty much was the extent of our communication all of the 7th grade year. Here we are getting ready to start the 8th grade and the only contact we had with a girl, even holding hands, was practicing kissing on our pillows.

The Unexpected Friend

It was great having a best buddy during this time. Going through puberty sucks but at least we suffered through it together. We talked about everything and made a pack to always look out for each other. We made sure we didn't have boogers hanging from our nostrils, our hair was combed but most importantly that our fly was always zipped up. Being a 13 year old boy was really weird. For some reason a certain body part had a mind of its own and you never knew when it was going to show up. We called it "Our Unexpected Friend." James and I had to look out for each other because we were both too stupid to even know when our periscope was rising. During this time in a boy's life, combining girls with boobies and the inability to control your physical impulses is just a disaster waiting to happen.

PE class was horrible because gym shorts don't hide anything so you always had to be on guard. This one time in gym class we had to climb the rope. James and I are both pretty athletic and we enjoyed playing sports, especially dodge ball. During this game we never threw at the other guys. We always aimed at the girls because at least we could get our frustration out at how they had this incredible effect on us.

Anyways, back to the rope climb. James had to go first and he starts to climb up. Being his best friend I'm holding the rope for him. He's dominating the rope and he's like 10ft up. All the sudden, the unexpected friend is starting to make a visit. I guess the friction of the rope set off the unavoidable reaction and his friend decided to show up. Here's my best friend dangling in the air with both hands holding onto a rope and he has no way to cover up.

Me and James always looked out for each other. So now I have to give James a chance to climb down and avoid the inevitable humiliation. I needed to create a distraction so I turn around and point up to the windows on the other side of the gym. I yell as loud as I could, "What the heck is that!"

I thought I did a good job and it worked, all the kids turned around…all except Gus Weaver. This jerk points up to James and yells, "That looks like a Boner!"

All the kids turn around and look up at James helplessly hanging there. They start pointing up and laughing at him. Girls covered their eyes and turned around and of course guys being guys, started chanting, "Boner…Boner…Boner."

I tried the best I could, I felt so bad for my best bud. Not to mention, to add insult to humiliation, for the rest of the school year he would be known as "Rope Boner."

Vacation with Us

After the trauma of being called "Rope Boner" all of 7th grade, I was able to convince my mom and dad that James needed to get away for the summer. He needed a chance to redeem himself and to get a new start for the big-time 8th grade year. If we were going to start our 8th grade year off awesome, we need to get a boost of confidence. And being called Rope Boner isn't exactly a boost to someone's ego.

My parents were fine with him coming with us. After all, he pretty much stayed with us nearly every day. He was a fixture at our dinner table and dad would even joke that he must have a food tab of over 1000 bucks. I don't know if his mom ever fed him because even in the morning when I'd come down to eat breakfast he would already be eating a bowl of Honey Comb at the table. But mom didn't mind…she thought of him as another son. What's odd is no one else ate Honey Comb in our house but mom would always buy a box for him.

Convincing his parents was pretty easy. Come to think of it, anytime James was at my house I always wondered why his parents didn't really call for him or come looking for him. I remember this one time he was hanging out at my house and we looked out my living room window and we could see his parents walking out with suitcases and drive away in their car. James didn't even know they were leaving. I asked mom if he could stay the night and of course she said yes. What turned out to be one night, actually turned into an entire week. I'm pretty sure my mom knew, but it was strange that James didn't know because he didn't even bring any extra clothes. Oh well, just meant we got to hang out longer.

Funny thing, when we were packing up James' suitcase, his parents were doing the same thing. And when we were packing up our car, they were doing the same. I asked James where his parents were going, he said something like Hawaii cruise. I asked him why they didn't wait for him to come back and have him go with them. He said they wanted to save money. But they brought his 2 younger brothers and sister with them. Even the dog went on the cruise trip and I don't even know if they allowed dogs. Oh well, it really didn't matter, we were about to head out and have the best summer vacation ever.

CHAPTER 3
Cousin Johnny

J ohnny was a cool cousin. He liked riding bikes, enjoyed playing sports, except he was a horrible athlete, but he tried. So anytime we wanted to feel better about ourselves, we would play basketball, tennis or even ping pong with him because we knew we would crush him. But he had a great sense of humor. As I mentioned earlier, he wasn't really the keeping clean guy, I guess he hadn't developed the curiosity of girls yet.

It was weird because Uncle John was like 6'3", had full head of hair and was athletic. Poor Johnny was shorter than me, had zero athletic abilities and worse of all, he had the receding hairline of a grown man. I swear, for a 13 year old he already had a bald spot on top of his head. He was really funny so I guess if you were dealt the cards he had, you better have a sense of humor. So at least now I wasn't the shortest kid around.

Johnny wasn't much in the style category also. It looked like his clothes were crumpled up in the corner and he would just pick up whatever shorts or shirts were closest by. Just like him, I don't think he ever washed his clothes. Either that or maybe he only had 2 shirts and 2 pair of shorts the whole vacation. Every day he was wearing his light blue or ugly green shorts and completing his unique ensemble with either an orange t-shirt or a hideous bright yellow shirt with the dumpy smiley face. At least he did wear red baseball hat to cover up his bald spot. I have to say, the kid had character and a great personality so even though his look was somewhat questionable, he was super cool to hang out with. He fit right in with me and James.

James and I were going through the weird awkward stage when it came to the opposite sex. Just last summer we didn't care what we looked like, we probably dressed the same way as Johnny. But now that we got the girl bug, we had to take our time to comb our hair, brush our teeth, and try to shower at least every other day. But most importantly we paid attention to our style. James and I were about the same size so we got to double our clothing outfits. If I wore my green Hulk shirt one day James could wear the same Hulk shirt but had to wait 3 days. We gave every item the 3 day rule. So this way by the time the other person would wear the item people usually would forget that it was the same thing one of us wore a few days earlier. We were smart like that.

So now that we got the girl bug, me and James set the goal that we were going to help my cousin out and make a goal that by the time our vacation is over, he would get the girl bug too. Besides, how could anyone start the 8th grade year and not like girls. By this time, the only reason me and James were looking forward to next school year was the girls. We couldn't wait to see Stephanie and Tiffany again and the next time we saw them, we were going to be ready to make our move. The saying "Hi" move.

Even though Johnny didn't really care, the three of us made a pack. We were going to actually speak to a real girl. Before the end of the summer, we were going to take the ultimate risk of uttering those two letters…"Hi." But we made a pack and somehow, someway, all three of us were going to be successful. At least we were going to try…well maybe.

Never before was it so difficult to speak to girls, heck just last summer we'd even play four square with them. But now that we got the girl bug, we got a frog caught in our throat and the words just couldn't come. Not to mention, our voices are changing so we had to do our very best to not screech or stutter. Being a boy and getting ready to start the 8th grade sure has a lot of pressure on it.

Clearlake Resort

CHAPTER 4
Clear Lake Family Resort

U sually in the summer, just our family go on a small vacation to a beach house, Disney Land or some other theme park. That was fun enough, but to spend the summer with my cousins was going to be the ultimate summer vacation. The resort was awesome. It was really big, surrounded by trees, a lake, beaches with a volleyball net and tons of outdoor activities. There were cabins and houses everywhere and all within walking distance. There were three pools and three clubhouses but the main club house had everything.

If outdoor adventure was our game we had a huge lake to swim in with a large platform dock in the middle of the lake. They had free bikes and fishing gear. We could use canoes, paddle boats, inner tubes and blow-up rafts all for free. We could go hiking and rock climbing. The resort even had zip lines that would crisscross through the trees and one even went out over the water and ended on the dock in the middle of the lake. In all my 13 years of life, I've never seen anything like this. Forget about riding the Matterhorn or Bumper Cars at Disneyland, we had everything an adventurous kid could do. We had something to do from sun up to sun down. It was paradise, especially since I got to spend it with my cousins.

When we finally get settled in, which is to say me and James ran upstairs into our room and threw our suitcases on the beds, we ran down the back porch stairs to go pick up Johnny and Uncle John's lame house. Johnny was finally done cleaning off his stink so off we went to explore our new playground.

The Arcade

Inside the main club house was also an arcade. The arcade was totally awesome, the games only cost a nickel but we told our parents the games were a quarter like back at home. This was smart thinking because the parents wouldn't have thought twice about it. So we had extra nickels and could play for hours.

Because Uncle John was pretty cheap, Johnny never really had quarters so he didn't really play games. How sad…this poor 13 year old never felt the joy of smashing a Donkey Kong barrel or chomping on a Pacman Ghost. We seriously felt sorry for him. So along with getting him to talk to a girl, our other goal was to introduce him to the world of arcade games. So with me convincing my parents that the games were a quarter it meant I had some spare coins that I could share with Johnny.

The arcade was a 13 year olds dream. At this point in our lives, we had started to spend much valuable time perfecting our Pac Man, Frogger and Donkey Kong skills. Back home, in between riding our bikes, playing butts up against the garage or baseball at the park, the next best place was at the local Sip-N-Flip pizza place. The food was nasty, but for a 13 year old, we had the stomachs of a Komodo dragon, so nothing fazed us. But the food wasn't the best thing about this place, the Sip-N-Flip had all the latest games so anytime we had a couple quarters to spare we would head off to improve our gaming skills.

In middle school, your reputation can be built on your mastery of games. We didn't do the pinball machines, those were lame, but Pacman, Frogger, Dig Dug, Centipede and Donkey Kong, those were our games. If you could get to the Orange screen of Ms. Pacman or the 3rd level of Donkey Kong you got serious street cred. And the ultimate would be to get the top spot on the leader board. You could look at almost all the games and find King James or Power Tony in the top 5 of leader board.

The arcade had all the games and even more the arcade stayed open till 11 pm so we could play outside all day and still have time at night to climb the leader boards. Because of our awesome gaming skills we knew that nobody at the resort could compete with us so we could get the highest score on the leader board in no-time. What girl wouldn't want to know who was Power Tony or King James?

We couldn't spend too much time inside the arcade, we just wanted to survey the layout of the arcade and plan our game quest strategy. Our goal by the end of our vacation was to have me, James and even Johnny get the top 3 spots on all the games in the arcade.

The Restaurant

The restaurant was really an all you can eat buffet. They would serve breakfast from 6 am to 10 am and lunch from 11 am to 2 pm and dinner from 5 pm to 9 pm. For each meal you can choose from just about everything you could want.

Every day the three of us would try to

experiment and see what the grosses food combination we could eat without puking. One day for breakfast we tried pancakes, with bacon, Frosted Flakes, syrup and oatmeal on top. We had to smoother with syrup because anything in syrup was tasty. I think the grossest thing we tried was spaghetti and meatballs with broccoli and mash potatoes mixed in. It was probably the broccoli that made it so gross, what teenage boy likes to eat vegetables.

Dessert was the best part. From the first time the restaurant opens to when it closed you could get all the dessert you could eat. They had every kind of dessert you could imagine; like 20 different cake options. Endless flavors of Pudding and Jell-O. Rice crispy treats. S'mores and ice cream, ice cream, ice cream. You could get all the soft serve ice cream you wanted.

We couldn't believe it. Anytime we felt like it, we could serve ourselves a chocolate, vanilla or swirl mix in a bowl, cone and even a sugar waffle cone. They even had whip cream, nuts and cherries to make Sundays or banana splits. Talk about paradise…if it wasn't for our mom's making us eat real food, we would have spent the next 6 weeks gorging and stuffing our faces on junk food 24-7.

Clearlake Resort

CHAPTER 5
Five Goofballs

Anytime my brothers and cousins would get together it was surely going to be entertaining. I would soon call Richard, Lee, Raymond, Ronald and Bill the nickname "the Five Goofballs." Up to this point they only got together for a few weekends a year. But now that they will be locked together at a resort surrounded by girls, lakes and any activity they could think of, it was only a matter of time before mayhem would follow these boneheads.

No matter what the activity was; Richard, Ronald, Raymond, Bill and Lee were going to find a way to take a normal activity into some sort of crazy ass stunt. Anytime when me, James and Johnny would see the 5 goofballs together we knew something was about to happen so we just liked to sit and watch for entertainment. At some point, whatever they came up with was going to be really cool or someone was going to get jacked and it would be the funniest thing ever.

Richard, Ronald and Raymond

Richard and Ronald were everything you'd imagine a couple of horny testosterone driven 16 year old boys would be. It didn't matter who it was or what the girls looked like, they wanted to go after them. It didn't help that these 2 combined had the brain capacity of a moron. The kids that wore helmets and rode the little yellow bus to school outpaced their IQ by at least 20 points.

Not only did they lack the necessary brain capacity to have common sense, they had the energy and impulsiveness of jackhammer just bouncing around. Rarely could they sit down in one spot for very long. So anytime they had the chance they were running amuck outside. Unfortunately for Raymond, he never seemed to care one way or the other, so he just went along for the ride.

Lee and Bill

Lee and Bill had both just graduated high school and were the oldest of all of us. This didn't necessarily mean they were the wisest, but compared to Richard, Ronald and Raymond they were Albert Einstein. They had no problem coming up with schemes and crazy ideas only to encourage the other three. With Richard and Ronald's impulsiveness and Raymond's inability to think for himself, the three of them were the perfect tools for Lee and Bill to have fun with.

If the three stooges had an epic fail, it was great because Lee and Bill would have a great laugh. If the three stooges were successful, they had something more daring to do. Basically, Lee and Bill were always in a win-win situation. They were never at risk and always ready to laugh. They were like the wizard the behind the curtain and they always knew what buttons to push to get the stooges to do whatever they came up with. You could say they were diabolical geniuses.

Demolition Derby

The resort provided free bikes so anytime someone wanted to go for a bike ride you would just go to the main clubhouse and check out a bike. One day the guys wanted to go do something with the bikes. The resort had all kinds of trails around so you could just get a bike and go riding for hours just exploring. But instead of going for a "normal" bike ride, these guys decided to see how far they can push the limits of these bikes. The bikes at the resort weren't like we have back home. These were more like cruiser bikes or something you'd see grandma's or grandpa's riding. They had big wheels and wide handle bars. You really couldn't jump, pop wheelies or do anything like that. They didn't even go fast enough to race.

The 5 goofballs didn't do any normal activity as normal instead they get the bikes and decide to play crash up derby. They rode around the lawn and smashed into one another. Actually it was kind of cool. Then they would try to kick and make someone fall off. And naturally when one would fall off, the others would try and drive over him. It was a mad dash if one of them crashed and fell to the ground. The other 4 four turnaround and drive as fast as they could to run over them. Of course Richard would be the one to get knocked to the ground. Unfortunately when he fell to the ground his bike kept going so it was far from him. After he hit the ground, Lee, Bill, Raymond and Ronald start riding right towards him. Richard tries to get up but it's too late, he was like road-kill on the freeway.

All four of them seem to get there at the same time. Boom, Boom, Boom, Boom…they all ran over him. Richard was finally able to get to his feet and goes to get his bike. You'd think with the other four already running over him the game would be paused until he retrieved his bike. But no, they turn and drive at him again. Richard starts to run as fast as he could. But for some reason he doesn't think about self-preservation like maybe climbing a tree, or jumping onto a table. No, this goofball still tries to run after his bike. It didn't take no-time before the others caught up to him and again…Boom, Boom, Boom, Boom. He gets hit and falls to the ground. He finally gets up and he covered with tire tread marks all over his arms and legs. But at least for him the other guys got bored and decided to try something else.

The Ramp

Now they wanted to try and jump the bikes and see how far they can fly. Like I mentioned, these weren't really the type of bikes that are meant to go fast, pull wheelies and especially jump. Lee finds a piece of wood and makes a ramp in the lawn. They do it a few times, and to our surprise it worked. Well I mean, it was more like the bikes just rode over the ramps.

The lawn outside our front yard was a natural hill that went down to the lake. The guys took the ramp and put it at the bottom of the hill so they could get more speed. It worked a little bit better, they went a little faster and jumped a little further. But still nothing like our BMX bikes.

The dock was not too far from our house and there was a walk path that led down to the dock. Lee came up with the idea to go up the path and see if they could jump the bikes into the water. Of course Bill thought this was a great idea, and then suggested they should get more bricks to make higher ramp. So they search around and find a longer piece of wood. They walked it out to the end of the dock and Bill put as many bricks as he could. When he finally added the last brick the ramp was probably 6 feet tall. Who was going to try it?

Richard of course always wanted to be the first at anything so he wanted to go. But then Lee said that he wasn't heavy enough and needed to add more weight to get enough speed to be able to jump. Bills tells Raymond to sit on the seat and Richard will steer. Hmmm…Bill and Lee look at each other and shake their heads like "no, it still won't work." Need to add more weight. So they tell Ronald to sit on the handle bars and with all three of them on the bike, they should definitely have enough weight to get enough speed to make the jump.

By this time a crowd had formed and were

watching all this take place. At the top of the walk path, these guys look like an episode of the Three Stooges. Raymond sits on seat, Richard is standing holding the handle bars and Ronald sitting out front with his legs dangling out over the front wheel. With a 50 foot path and a 50 foot dock with a 6 foot high ramp at the end, this obviously was a great idea.

Lee and Bill are standing and encouraging them saying you can do it.

"It will be awesome," they say.

In the meantime, they are busting up laughing, even before what was obviously about to happen. It doesn't take a rocket scientist to see the train from a mile away. The crowd now gets into it and start yelling in excitement. Either the crowd was just as brain dead as the three stooges or they were anticipating the greatest fail any of them have seen.

The Three Stooges take off and Richard is doing his best to steer. The crowd cheers as they start to go faster and faster and faster. Richard is actually doing a pretty good job of steering because he guides the bike down the path and onto the dock. They are seriously going fast now. Richard doesn't even need to peddle. Ronald is on the front and he can finally see what is about to happen. He freaks out and jumps off the handle bars lands into the lake. This causes Richard to lose control of the bike. Just as they get to the ramp his front tire is turned sideways and then…crash. They hit the ramp and the bike starts to flip over. Raymond who isn't holding onto anything starts to fly over Richard. Unbelievably Raymond's fat body actually gets high enough to clear the ramp and he lands in the water. At the least two of the Stooges landed safely.

But now it comes down to Richard. When Raymond is flying over him Richard completely loses control of the bike and flips over and smashes into the front of the ramp. He does a face plant and as if this wasn't bad enough, because he hit the ramp with such speed his momentum continued to him over again and flying into the water. However this dumbass never took his hands off the handle bars so now his flying into the water upside with the bike over his head. He lands into the water and the bike comes crashing down right on top of him.

The crowd erupts with oohs and aahs, screams and jumps with approval. This was the most awesome crash any of us have ever seen. I don't think Evil Knievel could have crashed better. Me, Johnny and James look over at Lee and Bill and they are rolling around on the ground laughing. They could not believe they just talked these three idiots into trying that stunt.

With the crowd in full chaos of cheers and celebrations the three stooges make their way out of the water. Richard's dumbass is still holding onto a now crumpled and bent bicycle and walks out of the water. He has a huge bump the size of a tangerine on his forehead, a black eye, is bleeding from his nose and is still covered in tire tracks from being road killed earlier. Needless to say…after that day at least Richard was finally smart enough to learn and didn't want to ride the bikes the rest of the vacation.

CHAPTER 6
The Pool

The resort had three pools on the property but the main pool was in the middle of the resort near the clubhouse. The pool was huge and was more like a water park. It had 2 twisting water slides and another water slide that had a 5 foot drop off. It had 3 diving boards; a 3 foot high, 8 foot high and a mammoth 20 foot high to test your nerves and skill if you dared.

The main pool was the most popular hangout for all the kids at the resort. There were over 100 homes or cabins at the resort so there we a lot of families there. Which is to say, there were a lot of girls. Since our goal for the vacation was to get enough courage to speak to girls, the pool was the obvious hot spot to be.

The problem is, girls at the pool wear bikinis and for a 13 year old, dealing with his "unexpected friend" this can be a challenge. Not only are the girls showing more legs then in our

PE class, they are showing more skin around their booby as well so this alone is giving us uncontrollable responses. How could we go into the ultimate hot girl's hub and keep our eyes from gazing upon things we've never seen before? In one way it was paradise, in the other way it was pure torture.

At first me, Johnny and James would just walk around the outside of the pool fence. We wanted to survey the area before getting enough courage to go into the lion's den. Everywhere on the pool deck is surrounded by girls, girls, girls and more girls. It seemed like all the girls were in our age range so this would have made our task even more difficult. How to choose who we want to try and say "hi" to?

Enter the Lion's Den

Me and James are feeling pretty good about ourselves because we have Johnny with us. At the very least, among the 3 of us we are way better looking than Johnny. So naturally we figure the girls will look at him and then look at us and know we are the better catch. We get to the entrance gate and make sure that Johnny walks in first. He's wearing his green shorts and red baseball cap to cover up his receding hairline.

James and I are strolling behind him. The gates close behind us and instead of just closing, it's like it slammed shut making a huge clank sound. All the sudden it looked like everyone in the pool just stopped playing and looked over at us. Man, now we have even more pressure. We no longer could just sneak in we had all the attention on us, so every step we took was going to get scrutinized.

Me and James start to panic a little and our hearts start to race as we see all these eyes staring right at us. We can't afford to not look uncomfortable or uncool. What happened in the next 10 seconds could impact our entire vacation. Being completely oblivious to his surroundings, Johnny just kept walking. It's like he was in his own world. I guess if you had the looks of him, you pretty much figured you didn't have any chance with any of the girls so you didn't care. James and I have to be on our best coolness and we start to walk behind Johnny. Our plan is working. We are strolling wearing our hats that match our shorts and with our towels draped over our shoulders rocking our Joe Cool shades. We definitely looked the part.

Johnny is leading the way and he spots 3 lounge chairs on the other side of the pool deck. This will make our journey a little longer, but hey, we are locked in. Johnny gets to the corner and starts to walk down the side of the pool. James and I are a few strides behind Johnny rocking our new flip flops. If you've never worn flip flops, they are foam sandals that fit on the bottom of your feet and a rubber piece that fits between your big toe and 2nd toe. Flips flops are pretty cheaply made and usually you would go through a few pair every summer. I'm walking on the pool deck and I get to the turn. I step with my right foot and all the sudden the cheap rubber piece that holds my foot in place snaps and I start to lose my balance. My foot slides out of the flip flop and now I'm seriously losing my balance.

Instinctively I reach out with my left hand and grab onto James' arm to catch my balance. But James didn't see what happened and didn't anticipate the grab so he didn't have time to prepare himself. Instead of him stopping my momentum and keep me from falling over, he loses his balance and my momentum pulls him towards me.

My foot is hanging out in the air and I'm trying to balance on the other. James slams into me and now we both start to fall. The whole thing is in slow motion. Here we both are trying to be the coolest guys on the pool deck and instead we smack into one another and are hopelessly falling right into the water. SPLASH!

Our hats fly off one direction and our shades the other. We come up from the water and everyone is laughing hysterically at us. Oh man…we went from the instant cool guys to the instant dorks. We both turn beet red but have to think fast and salvage our reputation. We have to play it off like we planned that so instead of jumping out of the pool as quick as we could, we just started to splash each other and play it off like nothing happened. To our surprise, it actually worked. The laughing stopped and soon after everyone went back to playing in the pool. We successfully held off the ultimate humiliation.

On the Pool Deck

Now that we have diverted disaster, we look over and see Johnny sitting on the lounge chairs. It's like he didn't even notice what had happened. Man this dude seriously is oblivious to the world around him. It's a wonder how even survived 7th grade.

After a couple minutes of playing it off, James and I climb out of the pool and head over to the other lounge chairs next to Johnny. We had to hang our towels on the fence to dry out but that's what everyone else did so it didn't draw any more negative attention our way.

We finally catch our breath and start to relax. Now we can officially start to survey the pool deck from inside the bars. It is way better to get an up-close look at the girls. These girls are hot…like Tiffany and Stephanie are hot back at school, but every girl here was like a Tiffany or Stephanie. We were seriously out of our element. We thought there would at least be an average girl that we could practice on. But no…every one of these girls was like a 10+ and they were going to test our courage limits. If we were going to get validation of our coolness and actually talk to one of these girls, we are going to have to be on our "A+++" game.

So me and Johnny are looking and trying not to point so instead we are using the goofy excitable head nods like "oh look at that one…look at this one." It was amazing we didn't get whiplash from turning so fast. For some reason every time we pointed one out to Johnny he'd just shrug his shoulders and nod like "whatever." Obviously this kid hasn't had the visit the unexpected friend. To be on the safe side, James and I made sure to not lay on our back, unless we put our towels over us. If we did want to go to the pool we had to make sure we were in a position to be able to walk. Dealing with the unexpected friend is torturous especially surrounded by all these girls in bikini's and bouncing boobies.

Obviously in no way are we ready to speak to the pool honeys, we could barely even look at them. But it is hot outside and we are at the pool so we might as well cool off with a swim. After we felt the coast was clear with our unexpected friend and it was safe enough to stand up, we went in and jumped into the pool. Swimming is great and you don't have to worry about looking cool. Everyone is jumping, swimming and splashing so we just blend right in. If you are confident enough to bring attention to yourself you head to the diving boards.

All three of us get out and decide to go to the diving boards. We all stand in line at the lowest level, jump out and make the coolest cannon ball. The cannon ball is a must when jumping off the diving board. And if you made a big enough splash to hit someone on the pool deck, you got mad props. So of course we are all trying our best. We made some good splashes, but nothing to brag about.

After a few tries we move up to the 8 foot diving board. Now this was getting little bit more challenging. If we jump off and get sideways or worse upside down, we could get smack right on top of the water. The pain hurt, but what's worse is when you get out of the pool you would have this huge red mark where the pool smacked you. It was unavoidable. So you had to make sure you were ready to jump off.

The safest jump is the pencil jump, where you just get to the edge, step out and fall feet first. This was common to do, but it was also the lamest way to jump in. If you were brave enough, diving head first was the ultimate but to get props you had to do at least do a cannon ball.

We have to build on our image just in case the girls remember our entry fiasco, we can't look lame again. We want Johnny to test the jump first so we put him in front of us. We watch him climb up. He gets to the top and doesn't hesitate, he runs and jumps out as far as he could, curls up in a ball and "SPLASH." Wow this guy is brave and for a little guy his splash was pretty big. Water actually splash landed onto the deck but it wasn't far enough to hit anyone, but for his first jump he was on his way.

Now the gauntlet has been thrown out, me and James can't lame out and do pencil drops, we have to cannon ball it. And more importantly we can't just walk out. Johnny ran on the diving board, so we have to do the same. James went first…splash, pretty good, I was next and not too bad either. We all felt confident so now we wanted to see who could get the biggest splash and get the ultimate respect. We kept going one after the other and even though we were doing really well none of us could get the right height, distance and force to make the water splash high enough to land on anyone.

The High Dive

After Johnny splashes again and climbs out of the pool he starts to walk to get back into line. But instead of stopping at the 8 foot board, he walks right past us to the most feared 20 foot diving board. Up to this point, only the adults had been jumping off the 20 foot diving board. But now we see Johnny walking to the ladder and he starts climbing up. Who is this guy? We thought to ourselves. For not really worrying about his looks, he didn't really care about heights either.

He gets up to the top. At least he is more cautious so he walks out to the end of the board. He looks down. He then takes a couple steps back, runs out and goes flying out over the water. He curls up into a ball and then…BOOM! He splashed into the water and even though he weighed like 50 lbs he caused a water explosion. The water splashed up high and far like a volcano eruption. The water didn't just go onto the deck, it went all the way to the fence and anyone in the eruption path was drenched with water. There must have been over 20 people that got doused on that jump.

You see the people jumping up on the deck and start yelling at Johnny as he proudly swims to the ladder and climbs out. The rest of us are all standing in line at the diving boards just staring at him in awe. He got all the pool props in one brave gigantic plop.

James and I look at each other and are like, dude we can't let Johnny out shine us. So we get out of line and walk over to the 20 foot diving board. It took me a few steps and I had just enough time to think, "What the hell am I about to do?"

No way am I gonna jump off the 20 foot board. I am afraid of heights. But now that I'm walking bravely to the ladder I have to think of something. I think quickly and jump up and start holding my foot. I act like I just sprained my big toe and now that I'm in pain people will understand that I couldn't possibly climb the ladder right now.

James looked at me and I said, "Dude you got this, I'll go with you the next time."

James was focused, he wasn't going to chicken out and come up with an excuse like me. I have to give James props, he was braver than me. James starts to climb up the ladder. He doesn't really like heights either but he's ready to take on this challenge.

He gets about halfway up but now the fear is starting to set in, which is totally understandable. But the worst thing you could do is climb down so he has to keep going up. To brace himself he pulls his body a little bit closer to the ladder and he slowly continues to climb up to the top. He is focused and keeps his eyes up to the top level. Unfortunately he doesn't look down so he can't see what is happening.

Oh man…just like the rope climb. James must have been too close to the ladder and he started to rub on the steps as he climbed up. He was too high up and I couldn't distract him because he may fall down. So from the ground I can see what is happening. The damn unexpected friend is making a visit. James gets to the top level, climbs up on top and what's even worse, he is so proud of himself for reaching the top and puts his arms up in like a victory celebration.

My best buddy is standing at the top of the 20 foot diving board, arms stretched out and yes he is in full periscope mode. The pool is filled with people and especially with the pool honeys. All of a sudden this one kid points up at James and yells, "BONER."

Then everyone turns and looks up at James.

They all start pointing, laughing and of course the knucklehead guys are yelling, "Boner… Boner… Boner."

All James could do is put his hands down to cover himself and get off the diving board as fast as he could.

James has no time to think or plan his jump. He just runs out, holding his goods and jumps off the diving board. Unfortunately for James, when he jumped he was leaning forward falling face first towards the water. To his bravery he could see what was about to happen but he still refused to take his hands off his goods to prepare himself. So he just closes his eyes and it was slow motion again. I'm staring at my best bud and feeling horrible for him. Not just because of his "visitor" but because I could also see the pain he was about to endure.

"SMACK!"

He hits the water face first in full on belly flop mode. The sound was so loud that even the dogs started to bark. Everyone at the pool became silent as they watch James in complete pain trying to catch his breath. In agonizing pain, he slowly starts to swim to the ladder. At least the thud of the belly flop took care of his unexpected visitor problem. James gets to the ladder and starts to climb up. The pool splash impact left his face and stomach as red as a tomato. Everyone on the pool deck is still silent and they watch him pull himself out of the pool. James reaches the pool deck and then the same knucklehead guys start clapping, pointing and of course start chanting James new nickname, "Belly Flop Boner...Belly Flop Boner...Belly Flop Boner."

Man, my best buddy can't catch a break. He went all 7th grade year of being called "Rope Boner" to now he's going to be spending his summer vacation with the new nickname of "Belly Flop Boner" or simply just "BFB" for short.

K
S

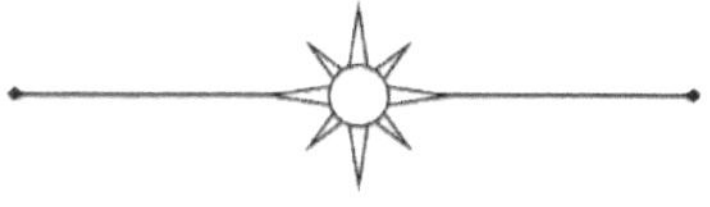

CHAPTER 7
Super Hero Sisters

My Big Sister...Kerry Krunch

Johnny and Sonya were close in age like me and my sister. Sonya also looked after him like my big sister did me, which is to say they were only allowed to beat us up. If any of the other kids in the neighborhood or at school picked on us, our sisters would quickly seek out to avenge on our attackers.

Even though they were girls, they were feared by all the other guys. I remember this one time when me and James were 8 years old playing catch in our front yard. There was an older kid my sister's age named Jack who loved to torment and bully all the kids on our street. Nobody really liked him but sometimes we would allow him to play with us because we felt sorry for him.

This one day when James and I are throwing the football in the front yard Jack walked over and asked if he could play. At first we hesitated, but since we were both together we could help each other if he tried to bully us, so we said he could. We are throwing the football around a few times and then when it's Jack turn to throw, all the sudden he turns towards James and throws it as hard as he could.

Even though James was a pretty good catcher, he was only like 5 feet away and the ball was too fast for him to catch. The football went right threw his hands, smacked him in the face and hitting his nose. Immediately his nose started to bleed like it was the Niagara Water Falls…blood was gushing out everywhere.

I ran over to help my best buddy but when I was running, the bully Jack tripped me. He took the football and again threw it as hard as he could in my stomach. After that he picked up the football and chucked it high up in our tree. He just laughed and laughed and laughed as he walked back home.

Now James and I are both crying lying down in our front yard. James holding his bloody nose and I'm curled up a ball like a roly-poly. My sister was inside but she heard us crying and came outside. She picked us up and walked us inside while holding James' nose. After my tears and snot bubbles had tried up and James' nose finally stopped bleeding, she asked us what happened.

We told her that Jack came over and threw the football at us and then threw it up in the tree.

Kerry walked outside and looked up in the tree. Jack really chucked it up there, it was like 20 feet up. She looked at us and told us to stay there. Kerry then walked over to Jack's house and knocked on the door. We soon see her and Jack walking back over and Kerry asked him if he threw the football in the tree.

He said, "Oh I'm sorry, it was on accident."

Kerry said, "That's ok, my brother is too small, would you mind climbing up to get it."

He was much bigger than us so it was easy for him to climb up there. He climbed up, grabbed the football and tossed it down. Jack jumped down and Kerry thanked him for getting the football down.

Jack smiled and said, "No problem."

It was almost like he was flirting with her…gross.

Then without hesitation Kerry hurled the football and hit Jack right in the face. She threw it so hard it hit him and he flew back like 5 feet and landed on his back. Kerry then picks up the football and while Jack is there holding his now bloody nose Kerry winds up and flings the football at him. But instead of hitting him in the stomach like me she aimed a little lower and hit him right in the goods. Wham, he rolled over with one hand holding his bloody nose and the other on his balls.

In between his crying and whimpers, he asks, "Why did you do that?"

Kerry looked down at him and said, "Oh I'm sorry, it was an accident."

She turned around and walked inside.

After this episode, word soon spread in our neighborhood and even at school not to mess with either me or James. I guess it would be sad that we needed my big sister to protect us. But in that instance of me holding my belly and James bleeding everywhere, we weren't thinking about how sad that would be. We didn't really have time to protect ourselves because of Jacks' ambush.

But even if we did muster up enough strength to fight back, there is no way we could have inflicted as much pain as my sister had. Needless to say, after that day we didn't have to worry about Jack playing football with us again, because he was too afraid to even walk on our side of the street and every time he saw Kerry outside…he ran inside his house.

Johnny's Big Sister…Sonya Smash

Johnny told us this one story that his big Sister

Sonya did. It was pretty similar except this time he and Sonya were actually playing together. He was 7 and she was 9. Even at 9 years old Sonya started to get the "don't mess with her reputation." She was a girl but also tomboyish. She didn't mind playing sports, riding bikes and most boy like, getting dirty. In my Cousin Johnny's words, "She was a cool sister."

Anyways this one day when he and Sonya are playing out front these three boys down the street were riding their bikes. All the kids in neighborhood rode bikes but on this day he and Sonya were playing 2 Square in the driveway. Sonya bounces the ball to him and he misses it. This wasn't a surprise because Johnny had the athletic ability of a 3 year old girl.

But anyways, the ball bounces out into the street and the three boys rode down to the ball. We thought they were going to toss it back to us. But instead they kicked the ball all the way down to the end of the street. It was a total jerk move so naturally Sonya yelled at them, "You Jerks!"

Johnny walked down to the end of the street and brought the ball back and they start back playing 2 square again. And again, Johnny misses the ball. And again, it rolls out into the street. The jerks ride over and kick it all the way down to the end of the street…again.

As Johnny would say it, "I look at Sonya and she doesn't say a word, she just looks at them. I know that look. I've seen that look. And whenever I did see the look I didn't know when, what or how, but I was going to get it."

She was like a stealth bomber and if you weren't on your guard like 1000% of the time, you were going to get it.

Sonya wasn't physical like Kerry, although she wasn't afraid to mix it up either, but Sonya was more methodical. She liked to plan her revenge. It's almost like she relished the opportunity to come up with the most crazy and unexpected plan of revenge.

So now Johnny goes back down to get the ball and as he does he notices that Sonya goes into the garage and grabs something. He wasn't sure what she grabbed and when he came back she must have hid it because he couldn't see where it was.

They keep playing for like 5 or 10 minutes and in between the bounces Sonya just keeps staring over at the 3 boys riding their bikes with "the look." The boys all park their bikes in their driveway and go inside their house. As soon as they do this, Sonya walks over to the bush, bends down and picks up what she must have brought out from the garage. A wrench. Sonya walked over to the boy's house, bent down and started to unscrew the front wheels on their bikes. I get it.

"She's going to make them mad and take their wheels off, that's cool," Johnny thinks to himself.

But no…this isn't how Sonya thinks. That would be too easy for them. Instead, she loosened the bolts just enough to not fall off. She comes back to our house and puts the evidence back into the garage. We start playing again and after about 10 minutes I started to get a little bored but Sonya wanted to stay outside bouncing the ball. Finally, the boys came back outside, picked up their bikes and started to ride in the street again.

Now is where Sonya would put her diabolical plan into action. Sonya stops bouncing the ball and runs to get her bike. She starts riding around on the street and then all the sudden she dared the boys that she could make a better wheelie then them.

Once a dare has been thrown down and especially by a girl, no boy can resist the challenge. It's the ultimate dare and if a boy didn't take the challenge it was worse than if he did and failed. You could never run away from a girl's dare.

So of course all the boys said they could and started to do wheelies. Every time they were successful Sonya would continue to dare them, "You can't do it again…. You can't do it again."

After the third or fourth try the bolts must have gotten loose enough because they all pulled wheelies at the same time. This time their front wheels fell off and rolled out down the street in front of them. They lost control of their bikes, crashed down onto the pavement and flipped over the handle bars. It was an awesome, gruesome crash. All three of them are lying on the ground reeling in pain and Sonya rides over to them.

Slowly she rides circles around them a couple of times, almost like she is admiring her victorious revenge. She looks down at them and says, "You Jerks!" and she rides back to our house, hops off her bike and skips into the front door.

I think they understood what had just happened. After that, those were the most feared words around the neighborhood and no one wanted to hear them, especially from my sister.

After hearing this story from Johnny, I have to admit that we both have the coolest sisters around. Not only is one to be feared physically, but the other is feared with mental anguish. The two of them together were the perfect invincible force of revenge. We would soon see this in the most ultimate fashion later in our vacation.

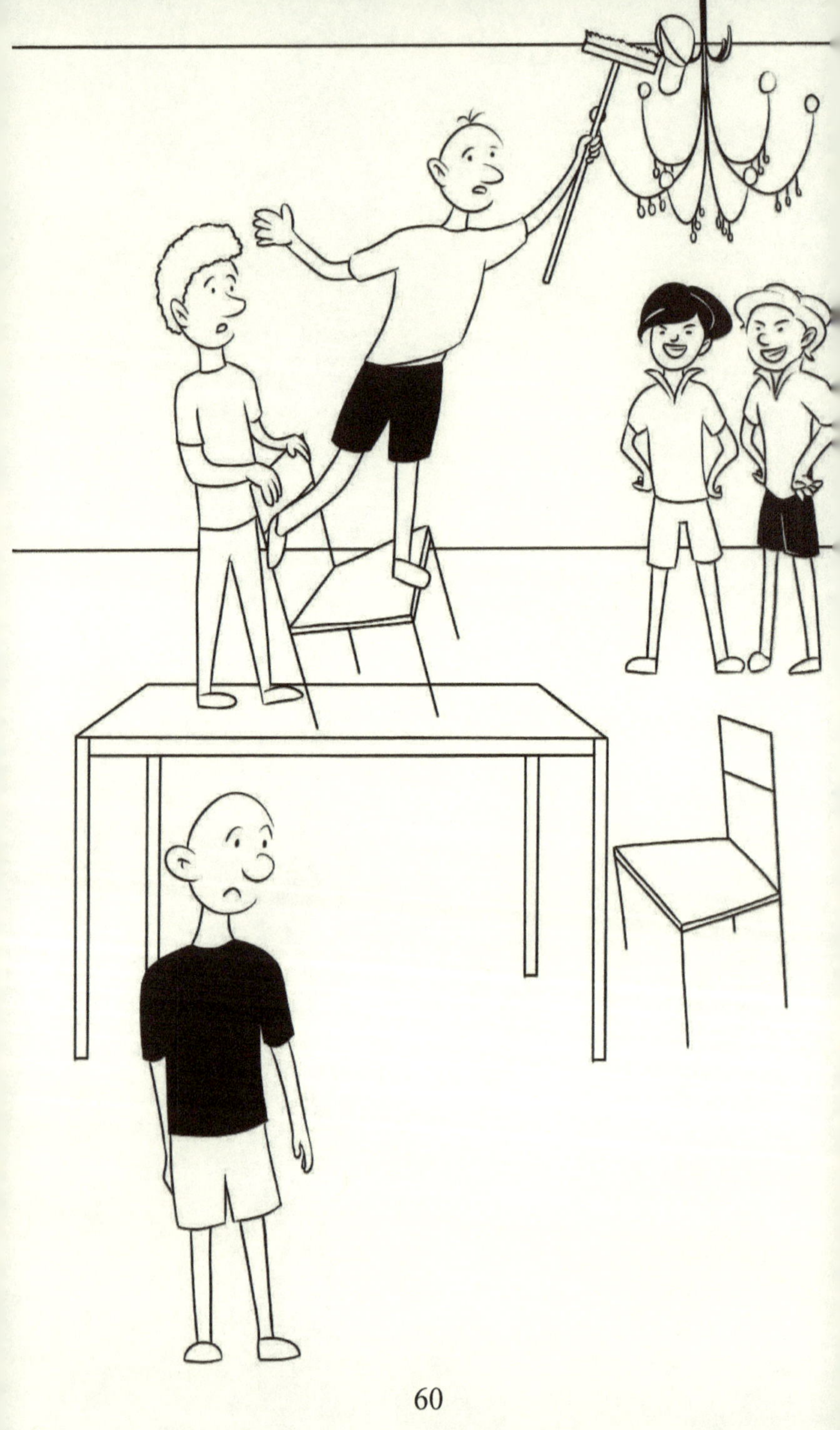

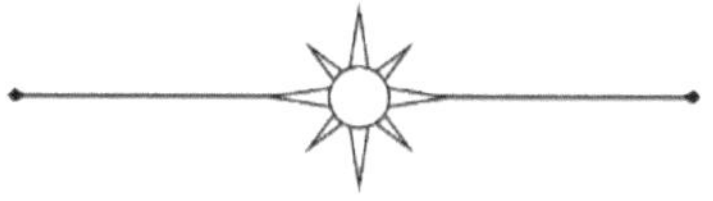

CHAPTER 8
Douche Bag Brothers

One day we when me, James and Johnny are in the arcade working on our Frogger and Donkey Kong skills these two older guys, like 16 or 17 came into the arcade. These guys were preppy looking with their creased white shorts and light blue and yellow polo shirts and penny loafers. Talk about Johnny looking like a dork, these guys were totally dressed like nimrods.

They came over and started talking to us. As if their outfits weren't hideous enough, they were named Darrell and Deaner Donaldson. To keep it simple for us, we decided to refer to them as the Douche Bag Brothers. Anyways the douche bags are standing around us watching us play. Right away we know these guys have no idea about jumping through the cars or smashing the barrels. They probably have never played a video game. Most likely they spent most of their time at their country club playing tennis, Frisbee or crochet.

James is battling the Donkey Kong gorilla and Johnny is watching me play Frogger and perfect the skill of timely hopping in and out of traffic. Remember I mentioned that Johnny wore a hat every day. He is just standing next to me minding his own business and then Douche bag Darrell asks Johnny if he could look at his hat. Johnny is assuming and doesn't really care too much about stuff so he says "sure" and just hands over his hat.

Darrell puts it on and starts to walk away. Johnny looks at him and wonders if he is going to give it back or just walk away. By this time, I see Darrell walk away and I say, "Hey, where are you going?"

James then chimes in and says, "Give him his hat back."

Darrell looks back at us with a smug look, takes the hat off his head and says, "What, this hat?"

James, feeling testy, says, "Yeah dude, why you taking his hat."

Douche bag brother number two Deaner then says to Darrell, yeah man give him back his hat. But we knew he wasn't being serious. He had this dorky smile when he was saying that. So Darrell looks up and he sees this chandelier hanging from the ceiling in the restaurant. He reaches back holding the hat and flings it up in the air and it lands right on top of the chandelier. Now from a throwing standpoint, this was pretty cool, but because it was the douche bag who threw it because he was being a bully, it was just a jerk move.

They high five each other, start laughing and Deaner says, "There it is kid, go get it."

Poor Johnny doesn't know what to do. He just looks up and stares at his one and only hat. All three of us are standing there looking up at his hat sitting on the chandelier and I put my arm around Johnny's shoulder. I could only imagine how he felt. It was his only hat, so he had no other way to hide his receding hairline bald spot...I mean that's what I would have been thinking.

I tell Johnny, "Don't worry cousin, we'll figure out how to get it down."

Johnny just keeps looking up and shrugs his shoulders. He didn't need to say anything, me and James understood what he meant.

Me and James start looking around to see how or what we could use to reach up and get his hat. The chandelier was like 20 feet up so it was going to be a serious challenge. We spot a broomstick in the corner and James goes over to get it. At first we stand on a chair but we can't reach it. Then we stand on top of the table, still can't reach it. Then we ultimately put the chair on top of the table and stand on the chair but we still can't reach it. The hat is just too high up, and unfortunately all three of us are vertically challenged.

About the time James is standing on his tippy toes with the broom extended high above his head Kerry and Sonya walk in.

"What the heck are you doing?" Kerry yells. "Get down from there before you kill yourself."

Sonya looks up and sees what's on top of the chandelier and looks at Johnny, "Is that your hat?"

Johnny nods his head and me and James tell them the story about Darrell and Deaner and what they did. I see Sonya's expression change and her eyes start to glaze over. I totally understand now what Johnny was saying about "the look." It made chills run up and down my spine and I think James may have even peed in his pants, and she wasn't even angry at him. Kerry sees a person working inside the clubhouse and asks if they could get the hat down. The person came back with the ladder, climbed up and got Johnny's hat for him. After Johnny gets his hat Kerry thanks the guy and then she asked what they look like. We told them they would be easy to find, just look for the two dorkiest guys at the resort.

It must be a sister thing because then Kerry looks at Sonya, gives a devious grin and then says, "Boys stay inside."

Oh man…this vacation is about to get awesome.

The Warning

So Kerry and Sonya walk outside and start to look for Douche bag brothers and since they looked so hideous it wasn't hard to find them. The three of us are inside the club house and watching with anticipation. What where they about to do? We couldn't wait to see because whatever it was it was going to be totally cool. Surprising to us, they walk up to the Douche bags smiling and flinging their hair. What the heck? Instead of beating the crap out of these nimrods they are totally flirting with them.

We did hear Kerry ask if they could leave their brothers alone and they said, "I'm sorry, we were just joking around."

Naturally these dork wads are excited that they have girls talking to them, and from a brother's standpoint, Kerry and Sonya are pretty good looking. So of course these guys would like them. Our sisters are standing there talking to them, laughing and touching the douche bags arms. It was totally gross to watch this. Finally, we say "whatever" and get up and go walk out to go find something to do. We had a lot of things we could choose from.

CHAPTER 9
Five Goofballs …Again

One of the coolest things at the Clear Lake Family Resort was the zip line course that went through the trees. You could climb up stairs to a platform and put on the harness and zip down to another platform. It was really fun. There were like 7 or 8 zip lines that crisscrossed one another so you had all kinds of directions to go. What was even cooler is that one of the lines went out to a dock in the middle of the lake and then after you would swim back to shore. It was really cool. At first you were nervous because you are flying out over the water but once you figured it out, it was really fun.

Me, Johnny and James are playing as well, but we are doing it the normal way. It was exciting enough for us. At first the three of us were too scared to try the zip line to the lake dock so we just stopped at the platform before it. After about the 3rd or 4th time stopping at the form Johnny all the sudden climbs up on the dock zip line and me and James just watch him. Is this guy crazy? He climbs up to the zip line and gets in the harness. Dude this guy is fearless. He steps out and whoosh he goes flying over the water and lands right onto the dock. That was really awesome.

Naturally James and I can't be shown up by Johnny so I convince James to go first, like usual. So James straps in and whoosh, off he goes and just like Johnny, lands right onto the dock. I can't let my two buds show me up, so I find the courage to get in the harness and to step out on the edge. I push out and off I go flying through the air with the water 30 feet below me. The dock gets closer and closer and I get a little nervous but then my feet hit the dock and boom…success. It was really awesome.

Because of the natural risky and thrilling part of zip lines the 5 goofballs were already drawn to the zip line course. They all get up on the platforms and start zipping from one platform to the next and ending at the dock in the middle of the lake. But just as usual, they simply can't do a "normal" activity. It doesn't take long because soon they decided to get more daring.

The zip line is designed for the rider to sit in a harness. Safety wasn't really a concern for these guys so none of them wore the harnesses anyways. I guess the risky part of falling 40 feet was more exhilarating. They would hold onto the bar with one hand and swinging the other like a cowboy.

Since they didn't have the harness they now thought it would be cool to let go of the bar "before" the dock and just splash into the water. Way risky for me, James or Johnny to try, but I have to say that when they decided to let go of the zip line over the water and splash down into the lake it was really cool.

After the bike story word started to spread around the resort. Now anytime the 5 goofballs were together a crowd would start to form just to see what they were going to be doing next. It was as if the goofballs have become the designated entertainment show for the resort. So a crowd has started to form with people sitting on the shore and dock just watching these guys and every time one would splash land in the water the crowd would yell and give applause.

I guess the thrill of potentially mangling yourself by helplessly falling to the ground from 4 stories up wasn't enough for these guys. So instead of just one person hanging on the zip line, they decided to double up. At least this way, both of the riders could get mangled together. Of course with the encouragement of Lee and Bill,

Richard and Ronald get onto one zip line together.

Richard and Ronald are standing on the platform together and holding onto one side of the bar. With the other goofballs cheering them on they step out and dangling high above the ground they zip from one tree to the other. I must say it was a cool site because they looked like Batman and Robin zipping from one tree to the next. They went all the way around the course and when they got over the water they splash landed. The crowd erupted so of course this just gave the goofballs even more motivation to up their game.

The guys zip through the course and get to the last platform before the water line. All five of them are standing there together and then Lee looks at Bill and says, "Man it wouldn't it be cool to see if we could three on the bar?"

Of course Bill naturally agrees and says, "Yeah, the crowd would totally love it."

But even from down below, we could see that Bill and Lee had that crazy diabolical look in their eyes. What were they planning now?

Richard and Ronald are already amped up from all the applause and Raymond didn't really think anyways. So Bill tells Raymond that he since he is the biggest one he should hold onto the bar and Richard and Ronald will hold onto his shoulders. Raymond at first looks like he doesn't understand, not surprising, but then Lee chimes in and says don't worry it will work. Too bad that the three stooges never really learned that anytime Lee and Bill would say something would work it didn't mean for their own good.

The crowd sees Raymond in the middle grabbing the zip line bar and then Richard and Ronald on either side of him. In anticipation the crowd starts to cheer and yell. Lee and Bill are holding onto Richard and Ronald's waist to help them balance. Raymond stands at the edge of the platform and one…two…three he steps and starts to go. When they take off, all the sudden you see Ronald and Richard's shorts get pulled off. Lee and Bill had held onto their shorts.

So now the three stooges, with Raymond holding onto the zip line and Richard and Ronald completely bare assed hanging from his shoulders. Richard and Ronald are flying through the air literally dangling and are hopeless to cover up until they get to the water. Of course everyone watching are laughing and cheering hysterically.

But Richard and Ronald are too heavy and start to lose their grip. They start to slide down Raymond and are desperately trying to hold onto his waist. The stooges are about half way over the lake when Richard and Ronald finally lose their grip and start to fall into the water. However, as they fall they are holding onto Raymond's shorts and when they fall, so does Raymond's shorts. Now Raymond is gliding bare assed and he finally let's go and splashes into the water.

All three are in the water, completely naked and now they have to swim back to shore. Naturally Lee and Bill are dying, this was one of the funniest things they could think of and it worked. So Richard, Raymond and Ronald get to the edge of the water and have to walk out of the lake covering their private parts. By now, this spectacle has become one to witness by all. As the three are walking completely bare ass you see people in the crowd snapping pictures and giving them standing ovations.

That was a great stunt…and a great prank at the same time. Years from now people still talk about the three naked guys that splash landed into the lake. And there is even a picture in the club house to immortalize them.

CHAPTER 10
Charlie's Angels

One day when we were in our usual spot of the arcade we look over and see these three girls getting ice cream. These weren't just any girls, these had to be the hottest girls at the resort. Could we be daring enough to talk to them? We haven't even practice yet. They were so hot that me and James lost our focus and stopped playing our Centipede and Q-Bert games.

The girls looked our age but not necessarily. They had the increased body parts that we've started to notice about girls now. They were eating their ice cream cones and sitting at the table. Oh man...we haven't seen any girls like them at our school. If we could get enough courage to talk to them then we would definitely be ready for Tiffany and Stephanie next school year.

Johnny is oblivious, I don't get it. He seriously

has not gone through the "unexpected friend" stage because if he saw these girls, there's no way he would be able to control himself. By now we've spent a few days showing Johnny the necessary skills of Ms. Pacman so he is practicing and doesn't even notice the girls. But me and James just keep staring, we can't take our eyes of them. It's a good thing the girls didn't us because it would have been difficult to explain the drool on our chins.

After about 10 minutes in which me and James could not avert our eyes, they got up from the table and started to walk our way. Were they walking towards us? Well not necessarily, the exit doors were right next to the arcade so they had to come our way. James and I are just frozen. With every step these girls take we can't take our eyes of them. All three looked like the Charlie's Angels; long blond, wavy brunette and short black hair beauties.

The Angels are getting closer to us and me and James still can't close our mouths. As the girls are getting ready to walk pass by us they fling their hair as if to draw even more attention…like they needed that.

They all smile, waved their hands and say, "Hi boys."

James and I have this complete dumbfounded

look and still can't close our mouth to utter the necessary response. About that time Johnny had just finished playing Ms. Pacman and he turned around waved back and said, "Hi."

WHAT THE HELL! This guy is shameless…and incredibly brave.

In one second this guy had accomplished our goal for talking to a girl and he didn't even mean to. And what's worse, he didn't have to try. He just instinctively turned around and said "hi" like he was talking to his neighbor back at home. He must have had dirt in his eyes, because if he had seen how hot these girls were, no way would he have mustered up the courage to utter those two impossible letters together. And especially no way he could have raised his hand to wave.

James and I just look at him, both in complete shock and in admiration. We have no idea that this guy has so much moxie. First the diving board, then this. Man, we have a long way to go to catch up to him. Who would have thought it…the smelly, bald kid with wrinkled up clothes got a "hi" and a wave from not one, not two but three totally hot girls. Have to say, we both were a little envious of Johnny at this time. But this also gave us courage, if Johnny could do it, then we could also.

So needless to say, after James and I were

finally able to clothes our mouths and blink, we look at Johnny and say, "Dude, what are you doing?"

"Saying 'hi,'" he said. "Why wouldn't I?"

Well he did have a point, especially since the Angels said hi first, saying it back would have been a natural response. Ok, so James and I put that info in the back of our mind, next time we see Charlie's Angels and they say hi, we have to reply back.

CHAPTER 11
The Bike Crash

For the rest of the summer vacation we tried to be wherever the Angels were going to be. We couldn't make it obvious, but every morning we'd go out on our deck and see if we could find them. This one morning after we woke up we thought we should go get the bikes and just ride around the resort to see if we could find them. Maybe we could see where their house was and try to wander over there and create the next "hi" opportunity. We were brave, but honestly me and James would still probably chicken out. If we do see them again, would we be able to have a normal look and not the dopey, mouth opened drooling on our chin look? If we saw them again, this would truly be a difficult task to achieve.

We are riding around the far side of the resort and as typical 13 year olds we start to be goofy when riding bikes. Even those these bikes were bigger than us and were slower and completely uncool, boys being boys we didn't care. We weren't as crazy as the goofballs, but braindead none the less. It starts out with James pulling ahead and starts racing. Well of course this brings out the competitiveness with both me and Johnny. So James is in front racing on the path and zipping in and out of trees and bushes and me and Johnny race right behind him.

James spots a trail between two bushes that goes up into the trees. Me and Johnny are right behind him and we're on his tail looking for the opportunity to pass him. James makes a sharp right, goes over a little jump, back down the path and gets further ahead of us. Johnny and I go down another trail and try and catch up to him.

For a little guy, Johnny can go pretty fast. Johnny passes me and catches up to James. James and Johnny are going at it and I'm just behind them. They are side by side on the path and there is a little bridge that goes over a creek that is right in front of them a few yards away. There is a family playing volleyball near the bridge so we have to be cautious going over the bridge. The bridge is really only wide enough for one bike at a time. James takes the middle of the pathway and squeezes Johnny off the path. Johnny is going too fast to stop and he splashes through the creek and loses control of his bike, smashing into a bush right near the family playing volleyball.

At first me and James are thinking that was totally cool, what boy doesn't like a good crash every now and then. The family playing volleyball stops and looks over at Johnny. Wouldn't you know, it was none other than the Charlie's Angels who were playing volleyball. They look over to Johnny all wrapped up in bushes and start to walk over to him. Here we had been looking for them all morning and by accident, literally, we found them.

James and I ride our bikes over to Johnny. The three Angels are all standing there by him and now the girl with short black hair reaches down and asks if Johnny is ok. He says yes and struggles to stand up. Now all of a sudden she extends her hand and helps Johnny to stand up.

Dude…not only did he successfully talk to a girl and wave to a girl, now he has actually touched a girl's hand! Even though it was in a helpful nature, it was still a touch. Now all James and I could do is drop our jaws, again, and be in total shock about what we are watching.

The other two Angels are looking at me and James.

"Hi," they say and give us a wave.

Oh my god, they did it again! And just like last time, James and I are standing there with our mouth wide open, staring and again frozen.

Johnny who is now standing up, says, "Thanks."

And she continues the conversation and she introduces herself, "I'm Kate."

Kate then points to the wavy brunette and says, "That's Jacklyn," and points to the girl with blue eyes long blonde hair, "and she's Farrah."

Seriously... the girls we gave the nickname of Charlie's Angels actually had the real names and looks of the girls on the show? I don't know if it was a coincidence, but to us, it must have been fate.

So James and I are still just looking at them and we try to speak but words just don't seem to come out. Except the only sounds that do come out are "Umm...umm..umm" or James trying to clear his throat like he's a frog.

Johnny naturally just says, "Hi, I'm Johnny and these are my cousins Tony and James."

The girls reach out to shake our hands. Here we are standing and still can't close our mouths, still can't speak and now we're expected to actually touch another girl's hand?

No Way! James and I look at each other stuttering and stammering and both say, "Uhhhh...gotta go.... Bye."

We turn around our bikes and ride away.

Johnny then gets on his bike, says, "bye" to the Angels and comes riding behind us.

What the heck is going on? We took an oath that the next time they say hi to us we were going to be able to reply back. Not only did they say hi, but they actually introduced themselves and even extended their hands to give us permission for physical contact.

Man, these girls were even more awesome and intimidating than before. The arcade thing wasn't a mistake, these girls actually wanted to talk to us. But besides Johnny, me and James totally blew it. We are complete boneheads and now they'll never want to speak to us again.

We get back to our home, and the whole ride none of us could speak. Well, Johnny was oblivious so it didn't really matter, but me and James are in even more shock than before. When we get off our bike we just look up and see if the sky is green or if pigs are flying. Because something is really weird at the Clear Lake Family Resort.

Clearlake Resort

CHAPTER 12

Douche Bag Brothers …Again

After our fiasco with the Angel's the day before we found it best to stay on our side of the resort. So we decided to go down to the lake and ride the canoes. This was cool because all the canoes and rafts were free to use, you just had to bring them back. So the three of us decide to share and get in one together. At first we ride out the dock in the middle of the lake and jump off and swim out there. The big dock was cool because it also had a twisting water slide like the main pool. The dock was pretty big and there were a lot of kids out on the dock.

When we get there we tie up our boat and climb onto the dock. We go over to the water slide and start to swim. We were having a good time until we hear, "Look, it's the dorks from the arcade."

That's right…. It was the douche bag brothers, Darrell and Deaner. They go over to Johnny and say, "Hey you found your hat."

And they start laughing again.

"Leave us alone jerks," James speaks up.

"Jerks?" they said. "Did you just call us 'Jerks'?"

"That's right, you guys are being jerks," I repeated.

This time, not sure which butt-face it was, but he grabbed Johnny's hat again off his head and flung it as far as they could into the lake. Poor Johnny just watches as it splash-lands in the water. His eyes get a little watery and James and I instinctively put our arms around him and said, "Don't worry, we'll get it."

James and I look at the Douche bag brothers and say, "Just wait, you're gonna get it."

"Yeah, yeah, yeah…whatever dorks," one of them says.

We get back into our canoe and ride out to get our buddies hat. The whole time Johnny just sits there, hoping we can get there in time before it sinks. We finally get there just in time because it was starting to sink. Thank goodness, because again, had we not been able to retrieve the hat, poor Johnny wouldn't be able to hide his bald spot. I reach in and get the hat and give it to Johnny.

"Thanks guys."

From the first day of our vacation the three of

us have created a brotherhood bond and no way where we going to let our best bud down.

We row back to shore and start to walk up the path when our sisters see us. Kerry and Sonya were always checking in on us. Like I said, they were the coolest sisters, so anytime they saw us they asked us how we're doing.

"What's going on kiddos?" Kerry asks.

Sonya looked at Johnny and he just kept his head down while his soaked hat dripped down his face.

"What happened?" she asked.

"Those Douche bag Brothers Darrell and Deaner is what happened," James said. "They ripped Johnny's hat off and threw it way out into the lake."

I said, "We got to it just in time before it sank."

Kerry bit her lip and slightly shook her head. She replied, "Oh really."

She looked at Sonya and they gave each other the look and finally we're going to see those jerks meet the invincible force of the revenge sisters.

Kerry and Sonya look out and see the dorks out on the dock. They decide to take a swim and head out to the dock. Yes…we are going to see the Douche bags get it. Kerry and Sonya climb out and walk over to the brothers. We're waiting for them to kick the boys in groin or punch them in the nose. But instead, they do just like before, they start talking to them, flinging their hair and touching their arms. What the heck is going on?

Why are our sisters suddenly taking these nimrods sides? What happened to our Super Hero Sisters, we thought they were our revenge enforces. After a few minutes we get sick to our stomach and we can't watch anymore. Again, we look up in the sky to see if it's purple or pigs flying.

This whole place is weird.

CHAPTER 13
Ice Cream

We decided to leave before we all puked by the disappointment of watching our sisters betray us. So we thought what better way to cure our sorrows than with a huge heaping bowl of ice cream. We go inside the main club house and head to the ice cream machine. Soft serve is the best and you can pour as much as you can get in the bowl. They even have little sprinkles that you can put on top of you ice cream. So we get our bowls and fill them as high as we could, to the point that it's almost spilling over the side.

We get our spoons and head over to the table. Eating and talking about our favorite subjects; video games and girls. Even though we were still afraid of girls, we loved to talk about them. And of course me and James are expert arcade gamers so we could talk for hours about Donkey Kong, Centipede, Ms. Pacman. James and I are far more experienced with the game department and up to now Johnny had the most girl experience. But he didn't gloat, even though he could have.

We just sat there teaching Johnny about the keys to timing your jumps in and out of traffic on Frogger or whatever game. By now Johnny has started to increase his game knowledge and was able to share in our conversation. At times he would confuse Q-bert with Dig Dug, but we didn't mind, we knew he was trying.

After about our third or fourth bowl me and James go back for fifths. Johnny was still on his 2nd bowl. I'm not sure if this guy understands the meaning of "all you can eat ice cream." But anyways, me and James get up and go fill up our bowls. We're at the machine and then all of a sudden who walks into the club house...Charlie's Angels.

Jacklyn, Kate and Farrah all walk in and they see Johnny sitting by himself at the table. They walk over to him and say, "Hi Johnny." And ask if they can sit down.

Johnny shrugs his shoulders and says, "Sure, if you want."

Gosh darn it.... James and I are stuck at the ice cream machine and the Angels are sitting at our table. We are filling up our bowls and have nowhere to go. We're just watching Johnny talking and the girls are talking back and laughing. It's crazy, because this guy like literally only says 1 or 2 words at a time and none of it is ever funny.

James and I just stand there filling our ice cream bowls and stare...again, and watch this craziness repeat itself. We are fixated on the table and totally impressed with Johnny. We forget to notice the ice cream is starting to fill over the edge of bowl. We are too late to turn it off and ice cream over flows the bowl, pours over our hands and spills onto the floor.

James yells out, "Ahhh." And this brings attention our way. The Angels look over and see me and James standing there with ice cream all over our hands and dripping on the floor.

All James and I could do is look back. We couldn't move and not sure what excuse we could come up with to get out of there. The only way to clean up was to go to the bathroom but we would have to walk past the table. The girls weren't laughing at us but instead were smiling and waving. We couldn't catch a break with these girls. First we're caught drooling on our chins, then we run away like fraidy-cats and now standing there with ice cream goo dripping all over us. It was embarrassing enough, but we also wasted our ice cream....

James and I look at each other, then we decided to finally muster up enough courage to take the ultimate risk…well not exactly. Instead we noticed the side door, wiped our hands on our shirts and ran out. After about 5 minutes Johnny came out and joined us. In what we've now become accustomed to, in Johnny typical fashion he didn't comment on our actions or even mention the girls, he just said, "Hey guys, so what do you want to do now?"

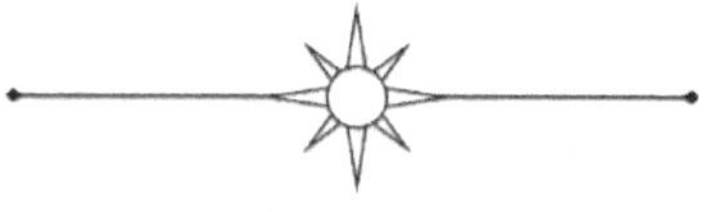

CHAPTER 14
Endless Torment

It seems like ever since we arrived and ran into the Douche bag brothers they would find some way to torment us. And since our big sisters have, all of a sudden, didn't get back at the bullies, this continued. Every time we see them coming we would try and go the other way. For the most part this worked but it became a challenge because it seemed like every day they were looking for us.

Even if we went to the pool on the opposite side of the resort they would somehow find us. We would try and stick up for each other, but these guys were pretty big. Even though they looked like butt-faced nimrods, we were simply overmatched.

Top Scores

One day we are in the arcade honing our gaming skills and building up our leader board. James and I have already made our way thru the arcade and we are both either one or two with the top scores on most of the games. By now, Johnny has learned a little and has even gotten his name on the top 5 leaderboard on Donkey Kong, which was impressive, because of all the games, Donkey Kong is by far the most difficult.

The coast is clear and we have no distractions from the Angels so we can focus in. All three of us are playing different games so no one is looking out for the Douche bag Brothers. Pretty soon we hear, "Look it's the little dorks again."

Darrell and Deaner walk in and start to do their usual jerky stuff. Calling us dorks and losers and whatever else but we are ignoring them. I guess this bothered them because they weren't getting our attention. All the sudden the games shut off...they turned the power off of all the arcade games.

Which doesn't sound like a big deal, but up to this point we have been spending hours and hours of climbing the leader board and now all of our hard work is erased by a simple unplug. For a 13 year old boy who has dedicated and committed the necessary sacrifice to reach the top three spots on Donkey Kong, Frogger, Centipede and Pac Man it totally sucks and is worst then getting your hat thrown on the chandelier. With one unplugging, Power Tony, King James and even Johnny Hairline (I thought of that one) are forever erased from the legendary status and no longer have bragging rights of owning the top spots.

The douche bags turn the power back on and are laughing and high fiving one another. What total jerks they are. The three of us are just standing there in silence just looking around the arcade. We're dumbfounded. Even now Johnny has learned the love of joystick madness and he is just as sad as me and James.

Soon after Kerry and Sonya walk by and see us standing in the middle of the arcade. They say hi and ask how things are going. By now we didn't care because we knew nothing was going to happen. "Doesn't matter," we mumbled while shrugging our shoulders then we turn around and walk out completely depressed. The whole thing just sucked…we all lost our high scores and our big sisters don't even care.

Bikes in the Pool

We found a good way to avoid seeing the Angels and the Douche bags by going to the pool at the far end of the resort. So this one morning when we got up we wanted to go swimming. We go the club house and get some bikes and ride over to the other side of the resort. There are always a few people swimming but not like at the main pool. When we are at this pool we're not worried about trying to look cool so we just play and goof off.

We're swimming, jumping and dunking each other and then go figure…who walks in, the Douche bag Brothers. We've been here for 2 weeks already and we can't get a break from these guys. We figure that they must make it their goal to finding us and tormenting us every day.

There isn't a lot of people on the deck and it was easy to find our stuff because Johnny's red hat was on one the chairs. They went over to our stuff and flung our towels and change of clothes and everything else in the pool. Except for Johnny's hat… Deaner decided to put Johnny's hat on his dumb oversized pumpkin fat head. They start to walk back out the gate, but before they did they got our bikes and pushed them into the deep end of the pool.

Darrell and Deaner are walking outside the pool and then we see our once Super hero sisters riding bikes nearby. They stop near the dufus dweebs and start to talk to them.

Sonya notices the hat and says, "Is that my brother's hat?"

Deaner replies, "Yes, he let me wear it."

Sonya knew that Johnny didn't let anyone wear his hat. It was like his security blanket.

Sonya says, "Oh, ok" with a glare in her eyes and then her and Kerry smile and ride away. Even though they have been laughing and smiling with the boys every time they've seen them, this time the smile seemed to be a little different, kind of a devious smile. Could something finally be happening?

CHAPTER 15
The Ultimate Revenge

Later on that night me, Johnny and James head into the restaurant to eat. We walk in and see Kerry and Sonya and they wave to us and say, "Hey little brothers."

Even though our big sisters have betrayed us, they were still our big sisters and we still loved them. So we walk over and say hi and chat a little bit. They were sitting alone at a table and we asked if we could sit with them, they kindly rejected us.

They weren't mean, they said, "Normally we would, but for tonight we're going to sit with some special friends."

We already kinda new who they were talking about so we just said, "Ok," turned and walked to another table. But before we did they told us to stick and that they will see us later on that night.

We're not really paying attention but then we see Sonya wave to someone at the front door. The Douche bag brothers, Darrell and Deaner

Donaldson, and Deaner is still wearing Johnny's hat. Can't believe the nerve of this jerk face…he is still walking around and showing off the fact that he bullied and stole a 13 year olds hat.

Since we first arrived these guys have been bothering us and up to this point, every time Kerry and Sonya would see these two they would just smile, flip their hair and laugh at their jokes. We seriously thought our big sisters had abandoned us and was going to allow the Douche bags to torment us our whole vacation.

So we see Darrell and Deaner Donaldson stroll over in their goofy penny loafer shoes, dorky creased white shorts, tacky light green and purple shirts (seriously what guy wears these colors). Kerry and Sonya are sitting down eating and they ask if the boys want to sit with them. Of course the Douche bag brothers couldn't resist so they went and got their food and sat at the table with our sisters.

By now it seems like all the families in the resort are inside eating at the restaurant. The whole time all four of them are laughing, joking and it's obvious that these two Douche bags are hitting on our sisters. This whole show was seriously making us nauseas. Before we would just walk away so we didn't have to witness the betrayal, but they did ask us to stick around so we were obligated to stick it out, no matter how gross this display was.

While they are at the table Sonya comments that she's always wanted to wear her brother's red hat. When Deaner hears this he takes the hat off his head and proudly hands it to Sonya like he's giving her a dozen roses or something.

Towards the end of the meal Kerry and Sonya ask the guys to get them each a piece of cake and a large glass of milk. By now, these guys would pretty do much anything our sister's had asked for so they jumped up and didn't hesitate to do this for them.

Me, Johnny and James are just watching this happen trying not to puke because our sisters have failed us and let these guys torment us. Throwing Johnny's hat in the chandelier. Throwing Johnny's hat in the lake. Unplug the arcade games. Push our bikes into the pool. Pretty much anytime we've seen these guys they have done something to us.

So now the Douche bags come back with the slices of cake and glasses of milk. They sit down on either side of Kerry and Sonya. Then we see our sisters look at each other. We've seen that look before and the three of us know what is about to happen. Anytime me or Johnny would have our sister's look at us like that, we knew we were in serious trouble. And just like with the three boys on the bikes or with Jack the bully, the Douche bag Brothers had no idea what was about to come their way.

Kerry and Sonya both stand up at the same time, pick up slices of cake and splat the douche bags right in their faces. The whole restaurant turns silent as everyone just looks at what just happened. Darrell and Deaner then stand up and start to wipe off their faces and they ask why? Big mistake in asking that question, that usually makes our sisters even more pissed off.

Kerry and Sonya look at them and without hesitating, "WHAM!" They kick them right in the balls. YES! FINALLY! The Douche bags are now both on the floor curled up holding their goods reeling in pain. Then Kerry and Sonya pick up the glasses of milk, clink them together as if saying cheers on New Year's Eve and then turn the glasses over and pour it all over them.

"Oh we're sorry, we were just joking around…YOU JERKS!"

The restaurant erupts in laughter and applause. I guess the Douche bag brothers had been bothering everyone else also. After a few minutes the brothers are finally able to get to their feet. They stand up, covered in cake and milk dripping all over them and while still holding their goods start to walk out of the restaurant.

Everyone continues to cheer as the brothers take the ultimate walk of shame.

The dorkwad dufus butt-faced Darrell and Deaner Donaldson, the Douche bag Brothers, just met the invincible force of Kerry Krunch and Sonya Smash. Needless to say, they didn't bother us again. In fact, they must have cut their vacation short, because no one saw them after that day.

Kerry and Sonya must have been planning the revenge ever since the hat in the chandelier episode. Our sisters come over to our table and Sonya puts Johnny's hat back on his head and Kerry says, "That's for you little brothers."

Apparently they didn't just want to get the Douche bag brothers back for bullying us, they planned to humiliate them in the most ultimate fashion, in front of the entire resort.

Me, Johnny and James just sat there in awe of our Super Hero big sisters. Admiring the devious planning and execution of the ultimate revenge. But we also became more deathly afraid. After that day we never wanted to get that look, especially when they were together.

Kerry and Sonya's reputation spread throughout the resort and just like back home, we didn't have to worry about anyone bother us anymore, and just like back home, we didn't care if our big sisters protected us.

S
K

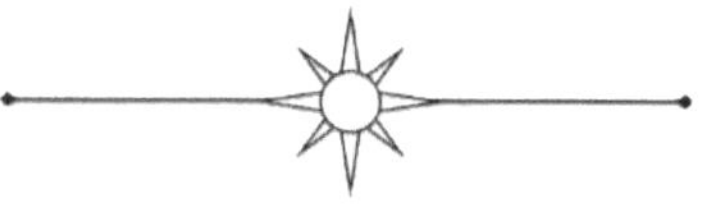

CHAPTER 16
We Meet

A couple days after the restaurant ultimate revenge Kerry and Sonya came up to us and asked if we wanted to go hangout with them. This was a little unusual but hey, these are our big sisters and after what they did to the Douche bags why wouldn't we want to hang with them.

The resort had beach volley ball nets and there were all kinds of games going on. It was pretty cool because teams would rotate and play against new opponents. We played together as a team and because we were an athletic family (except for Johnny) and especially because me and James are awesome we dominated every team we played. As we're crushing yet another team, we notice that at the far net the Angels were playing also. Pretty soon as teams rotated we would ultimately end up facing off against the Charlie's Angels team.

When the Angels see our sisters, they say, "Oh my gosh, you two are the ones that beat the crap out of those boys in the restaurant. That was totally awesome."

Kerry and Sonya just smiled and then Sonya says, "Have you met our brothers."

The Angels smiled and then say, "Well kinda, we haven't really talked much."

But who cares, it wasn't time for introductions and being nice, we're about to play volleyball and now it was time for us to take our frustration out. We start to play and at first, just like all the other teams we start to crush them. But to our surprise the Angels are actually pretty good. They didn't play like typical "girls," they took it serious and were competing with us. They were jumping high and diving in the sand and fighting back to make it a game.

Competition brings out the best of me and James, so just like in dodge ball we didn't care that we are playing the totally hot Charlie's Angels, we wanted to dominate them so no way were we going to let down. It's all about winning for us. This was our last and best match of the day so naturally we ultimately won. After the game me, James and Johnny are high fiving ourselves in victory. We see Kerry and Sonya talking to the Angels. They are probably bragging about our awesome victory. It didn't matter, at that moment we got to make up for the fiascos of the arcade, ice cream and bike crash episodes.

The Dock

Sonya and Kerry come back and tell us that they want to go swim out to the dock and cool off. Of course, what better way to celebrate a victory then swimming. So the five of us all jump in the canoe and paddle out to the dock. We are in full on celebration mode doing back flips into the water, jumping off the water slide and goofing off in general. Basically acting like 13 year old boys. It was cool because for some reason, the five of us had the whole dock to ourselves. Pretty soon we start to see three people in a canoe paddling out to the dock. This wasn't really a big deal, just meant we wouldn't have the dock to ourselves.

Except, this wasn't just three people, the closer the canoe got the more we could see who it was. It was Charlie's Angels. That's right, Jacklyn, Kate and Farrah are on their way to the very dock we are at. They get to the dock and Kerry and Sonya go over to them and smile and say hello. Then Kerry and Sonya do the unthinkable, they take the girls hands and walk over to me, Johnny and James and say, "These are our brothers."

Then to make matters worse, Sonya points to me and tells me to introduce myself. I take a deep breath and utter the words I've never been able to speak up to this point, "Hi, I'm Tony."

Then Kerry points to James, who does the same and of course Johnny has already taken the big leap and didn't need to introduce himself again but Johnny being Johnny says, "Hi, I'm Johnny."

Well, at least we were finally able to reach our goal of finally saying "hi" to a girl, even though it took our big sisters to help us out. Sonya all of a sudden smiles at the three of us and says, "Ok boys, we're taking the canoe back so you're on your own."

Sonya and Kerry then get in the canoe and standing at the dock we hopelessly watch them peddle back further and further away from us. It finally hit us, our big sisters must have been planning this the whole day. They really are devious. Not sure how, but they figured out that we have been trying to talk to the Angels ever since the first time we saw them at the arcade.

There we are, standing all alone on a dock in the middle of the lake with Charlie's Angels across from us. We are literally stuck staring at the girls directly across from us with nowhere to hide or run to. Johnny being Johnny just says, "Hey girls, that was a good volleyball game."

Farrah breaks the ice and says, "Your sisters are totally cool."

And naturally we couldn't disagree and that starts the whole conversation.

We started talking and me, James and Johnny told them all the awesome stories about our big sisters. It was a bonding moment. The Angels especially loved the Jack story. We talked about the Douche bag Brothers and the girls even had their story to share about those jerks. Crazy how those guys literally tormented everyone at the resort.

What started out with a couple of stories turned into full-on conversations and before we knew it we noticed the sun started to go down. All six of us are just hanging out on the dock talking together like we are all knew each other for years. We must have been out there for hours. We found out that the Angels were all best friends and were about to start the 8th grade just like us. They were vacationing with their families as well but were staying the whole summer. They said their family had been vacationing at the resort for the past 5 years. I could only imagine how cool that must have been.

The sun was going down so we decided that we should start to head back. By this time, me, James and Johnny had been talking to all the girls so we really didn't know who we liked or didn't like but most importantly we didn't even know if they liked us. And if they did, who liked who? Usually with guys there is a pack when their group meets a group of girls. We let the girls decide. If girls are interested they can easily show this by either talking to a guy directly or most obviously, sitting next to him. But up to this point we all had been sitting together on the dock so we didn't really separate ourselves.

Since we are the guys, it's our job to take the oars and row the canoe back to the shore. James sits at the front, Johnny in the middle and I'm at the back of canoe. This creates a natural separation so now the girls can decide where to sit. If they all sit on one seat then we know they are not interested in any of us. But all the sudden, Jacklyn sits up front with James, Kate sits next to Johnny and Farrah sits in the back with me. Bingo...the mystery is solved, not only do we know the girls like us, we know who they like.

With smiles on our faces, me, James and Johnny all proudly row back to shore. We've spent hours hanging out and talking to girls, real girls. We get back to shore, pull the canoe up and all get out. We stand there in silence for a few minutes not sure of what to do so now there's awkwardness. Johnny being Johnny blurts out, "Ok, goodnight."

And turns and starts to walk up the hill. Ironically, at this point Johnny has become our impromptu leader amongst the girl category so me and James look at the girls, wave and say goodnight.

We walk up to our house high fiving and celebrating that we fulfilled our goal of talking to girls. Not only did we talk to real girls, we talked to the hottest girls at the resort. As we get to our house we see our sisters sitting on the porch swing and smiling at us. It's like they were waiting for us to return. "Hey brothers, did you have a good time?"

They had a sly grin that they knew all along what they were going to do from the moment they woke up in the morning.

Of course we couldn't hold in our excitement. We spent the next hours just talking with our big sisters and listening to their advice of how to talk to a girl and to be respectful and nice. It's weird because even though they were girls, they seem to know everything about how a boy should act. It was a totally cool bonding moment for all of us.

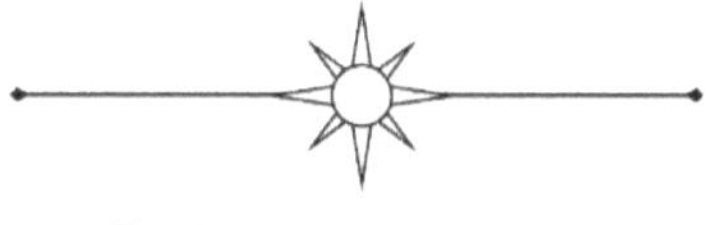

CHAPTER 17
Girlfriends

The next day we couldn't wait to go meet the girls at the main club house get our day started. From that day the six of us were inseparable. Go on bike rides, hanging out at the dock, riding the zip line course and even at the arcade. Our day would start with all of us meeting in the restaurant for breakfast. We would then make the plan for the day. And the cool thing about being a teenager, just like talking on the phone, you could just spend hours doing nothing but it's actually something. Some days we would just go sit down by the lake shore or under a tree. As long as we were all together it didn't matter. For us, just the fact that we had something to look forward to everyday was great.

We even got to meet their family and anytime we would have a BBQ the girls were with us. They became part of our group and Sonya and Kerry became our care takers. Anytime they would see the girls they would always ask if we are being respectful to them. They wanted to make sure that we were listening to their advice but also it was their way to let the Angels know that they were looking out for them as well.

As we start to get to the final few days of our six week vacation our time together would start to carry a deeper meaning. By this time all of us have taken the big leap of actually holding hands together. Johnny of course was indifferent and probably did it because Kate grabbed his hand first, but for me and James, we had exceeded our summer goals. We met girls, talked to girls and now are even holding a girls hand.

For some reason, during this whole time James and I never really spoke about the upcoming 8th grade year and Stephanie and Tiffany never came across our mind. How did this happen? From the last day of school the whole goal for our summer was to get ready and come back ready to talk to them. But now things really were different. We didn't just meet girls, it seemed like we actually had girlfriends.

But you can't really claim to have a "girlfriend" until you do the unthinkable and riskiest thing you could do with a girl…the kiss. Up to this time this thought didn't really cross our mind, but as we got to the last couple of days James and I started to talk about it. Did we really have enough courage to try it? If we were ever going to have an opportunity to have our first kiss it would be with the Angels. Maybe they were thinking about the same thing we thought. The more we talked about it the more nervous we got even speaking about it. Johnny of course was not helpful, because he didn't really care. But James and I couldn't stop thinking about it. Could we finally be able to actually kiss a girl? If somehow we could get enough courage to even try and be successful, this would be the most incredible summer vacation ever.

The last day we spent at the resort all six of us knew the next day was going to change. I guess spending this much time together you start to develop feelings. It's different then spending a weekend together, spending a month together really impacts how a person feels. Especially for a teenage boy and girl who have spent almost every hour of the day for the past 4 weeks together talking, holding hands and pretty much just being around each other. But now it was our last night.

Underneath the Stars

We wanted to spend our last sunset together so

we all decided to go out to where we actually first met, the dock. Kerry and Sonya must have sensed something because when they saw us standing on the shore for some reason they came out and walked down to us. By now they have pretty much become the big sisters for the Angels also so they gave all the girls a hug. Then Kerry and Sonya look at me, James and Johnny, gave us a weird smile.

They nodded their head and said, "You'll be fine, go have fun."

We didn't know what our big sisters meant, but we would soon find out. The six of us walked down to the canoes but instead of all of us getting into one canoe, each couple got their own.

As we start to row out we are all laughing and talking but as we get closer to the dock we all stop talking. It's as if there was a sense of anticipation. We've probably come out to the docks 50x before but for some reason things were feeling a little bit different.

We get to the dock and all sit down together. No-one is talking, we are just watching the sun going down and then soon we can spot the stars starting to show themselves. We are all sitting together and a little awkwardness is in the air. Where we all thinking the same thing and no-one knew what to do or what was going to happen.

Then all the sudden, Kate leans over to Johnny, puts her hands on his face and pecks him right on the lips! Wow, this guy beat us to everything. Of course Johnny would have been the first one to get a kiss because he didn't really care one way or the other. He was just lucky because Kate grabbed his face and made him kiss her.

But actually this made the rest of us even more tense. Me, Farrah, James and Jacklyn are still holding hands just watching Kate and Johnny kissing. Again, Johnny didn't really care, but since Kate wanted to, he just kept doing it.

I can feel both me and Farrah's hand sweating together. Would we actually kiss? I knew she was just as anxious as I was. I'm nervously looking around trying to make it look like I'm staring at the stars. But then out of the corner of my eyes I see James lean in and give Jacklyn a kiss. Oh my gosh…now my two best buds have done the unthinkable, they both kissed a girl. They weren't practicing on a pillow, they planted their lips on a real live girl. Wow!

I have no idea what to do…I just keep looking up, then I turn and look at Farrah. She looks at me with her long blonde hair and big blue eyes, I scratch my head, give an uncomfortably scared grin and then look back up at the stars. I seriously was way too scared to even try. Getting rejected by a girl can be the ultimate humiliation for a teenage boy. But getting a first kiss from a girl can be the ultimate reward, the dilemma one faces.

Farrah must have known my nervousness, like it wasn't that obvious, so instead she just scooted a little closer and put her head on my shoulder. For the rest of the evening, we looked up at the stars and occasionally glance over at our best friends kissing. But it didn't really matter, we shared our last sunset the way we wanted to. No pressure, just the two of us sitting together with her head on my shoulder and my arm wrapped around her.

At the Steps

I'm sure we all would have liked to stay all night out on the dock but after a few hours we finally decided it was time to go back to shore. We paddled back and walked up the shore together. By this time, we have learned the etiquette of walking our girlfriends to their home. We are all walking hand in hand and finally arrive to the sidewalk leading up to their house. By now Johnny, Kate and James, Jacklyn have already figured out the art of sucking face. But this didn't bother me and Farrah nor put more pressure on us.

Me and Farrah start to walk up the path still holding hands and we get to her front porch. Time is now frozen and I can feel my heart beat pounding inside my chest. We are staring at each while holding hands and then I go to give her a hug. As I'm leaning in to wrap my arms around her, she turns her face and kisses me on the cheek. Oh man, I move my head back and see her big blue eyes wide open staring back at me. Could this be the moment? If I ever had permission to go for a kiss it would be now. I take a deep breath. It feels like my heart is going to burst it's beating so fast. I slowly pull my head towards hers and she pulls her towards mine. As our mouths get closer and closer we both close our eyes and then smack…we hit our foreheads. After the ultimately fail…we both laugh, keep looking at each other. So we try it again but this time with our eyes still open we lean in and kiss on the lips. YES!

I step back still holding her hands. Her big blue eyes still looking right at me. I just kissed a girl on the lips! I'm thinking to myself. Who cares if we were the last couple to kiss and who cares if we bumped our heads in the process. We smile at each other like we both just did the most awesome thing ever. But the kiss didn't satisfy us, now that we broke through the pressure we wanted to try again…and again…and again. It seemed like we spent the rest of the night embraced in a kiss with her arms wrapped about my neck and my arms on her waist. It was the most incredible experience I've had in my life.

Finally we see the girl's porch light turn on and off and back in these days it meant it was time to go inside. So all of us give one last kiss goodnight and the three of us all turn and start to walk back home. Except we didn't need to walk back home, it felt like we were floating back on clouds. We get to our front yard and Kerry and Sonya both walk outside to meet us. They could see our smiles from ear to ear and the goofy glaze in our eyes. They must have known something. They looked at us, gave that strange grin again. They put their hands on our cheeks, gave us all a peck on the forehead and then said, "Good job little brothers, we're proud of you."

We stayed up all night just talking about what had just happened and Kerry and Sonya wanted to know everything about it. They especially wanted us to talk about how we felt and what it meant to us. They instinctively knew something had changed with us. We have officially crossed over into the world of feelings.

Up to this point the only feelings we had were when it hurt getting hit in the nose with the ball or the feeling of cuts and bruises when we crash our bikes. But there was a weird feeling that we couldn't really understand. We felt warm inside and our heart felt like it could explode with joy. Even if we tried, we could not make our goofy glaze or smile go away. It was like we were in a trance…a love trance. Kerry and Sonya just told us to cherish this feeling and embrace it forever. It is what life is all about they would say.

Our big sisters always looked out for us. They protected us from bullies and they gave us the courage to take big steps in our young lives. And if we were too afraid, they would simply put us in the situation to make it happen. It took us a long time to figure out why our big sisters wanted to hang with us that day, but if they didn't make us, none of these big steps would have ever happened.

CHAPTER 18
Longest Walk Home

The next morning started and we had to get ready to pack. The smiles had disappeared and trance had worn off. The warmth inside our heart started to turn into a panic. Why did we have this queasy feeling inside our stomach. We finish packing and carry our luggage out to the cars.

Me, James and Johnny look over and we see the three Angels walking towards us, by now we can officially call them our girlfriends. Kerry and Sonya see them first and go over and talk to them. We're not sure what they are saying but then Kerry and Sonya give all the girls a hug and then just like the very first time on the dock, they walk with them down to us. For some reason Kerry and Sonya have tears in their eyes and they kiss our foreheads and they walk away.

We look at Farrah, Jacklyn and Kate and they all have tears forming in their eyes and then we finally get it. Tears start to flow from ours. Here we stand together looking at each other and holding hands for what we knew would probably be the last time ever. Unfortunately we could only have a few minutes but if we could have, we would have never let go of our hands. The six of us have become boyfriends and girlfriends and we all shared the greatest first experience a kid can have together. So we all had the very same feelings and emotions that will forever link us together.

After a few minutes my mom said it was time to go but then Kerry and Sonya look over at mom and said that we needed to walk the girl's home. Mom agreed and then said to take our time. So we turn and take our girlfriends hand for one last walk. Holding hands together and regretting every step we took because it meant we were getting closer and closer to their house.

Farrah and I get to the walk way and stare at the path that leads to her front porch. It all started there. Just last night our lives changed forever, and now with these 10 steps that we are about to take our lives will forever be changed again. We both just stand there looking at the path and neither one of us wants to take a step.

Begrudgingly I take the first step and we walk as slow as we can. Our hands are tightly held together like we are trying to hold on for eternity. We get to her porch and turn and look at each other. By now tears are streaming down both of our faces.

We had our last sunset, we now had our last walk and now we have our last time to hold each other's hand on their front steps. I look at Farrah and just stare into her big blue eyes with tears rolling down her face. I lean in and give her one last kiss. This wasn't the type of make-out kiss, this was the small sad kiss that one shares when they know the time has come to an end. After our peck we simply put our heads together as if by instinctually replaying our very first kiss. It felt like vice grips needed to pull me away but it was time to walk back.

My heart hurt…my stomach hurt…I couldn't speak because the lump in the throat wouldn't go away. My legs felt like a 1000 pounds and I could barely make them move. But it was time to finally leave. With the girls all standing on the front porch me, Johnny and James start to walk down the path.

The three of us can't look at each other because we all must have felt the same thing. Just the night before we were flying back home, now it seems like we are walking back through quick sand. We get a few steps down the path and for some reason I need to turn around for one more look. As if we are all in unison, the three of us stop and turn around. I guess they wanted one last look as well.

We see Jacklyn, Kate and Farrah still standing on the front porch with tears streaming down their cheeks. By now the three of us were crying as well. And just like the very first time we saw them, they smiled and gave us a wave. But unlike that first time for me and James, all three of us smiled and waved back. We didn't need to be afraid anymore, we had girlfriends…. We had Angels.

We turned back around and started to take the longest walk of our young lives. Even though we were all three together, it was the quietest and loneliness walk we've ever had. We couldn't talk but you could hear each other's sniffles. We get to our front yard and there standing with open arms are the best biggest sisters in the world.

Kerry and Sonya walk over and wrap their arms around all three of us in a big group hug. I guess the feeling we couldn't understand was the hole in our heart we would now feel. They knew it was coming and they knew what we needed in that very moment. We needed our big sisters to protect us and comfort us like they always had before. Only this time they were sharing tears with us.

Then Sonya and Kerry pick up our chins, kiss us on our foreheads, look into our tearing eyes and just say, "You will be ok…you will be ok."

It's amazing how your heart can get so full ready to explode with joy and love to have the same explosion turn to hurt and pain. The night before, we were floating in the clouds with a goofy glaze in our eyes and a heart full of love. Now it feels like we are being dragged through the concrete and our once full heart has been shattered into a million pieces.

Bob's Bar
Bob's Bar
BEER
OPEN

CHAPTER 19
Bob's Bar

In the summer of 1982, my family went to the Clear Lake Family Resort in what turned out to be the best summer vacation I ever had. It was such an awesome time to be able to spend it with our cousins. We all promised each other that we will have to get together again next summer and to keep the tradition going. But as time moves on and life changes occur unfortunately that would be the only summer vacation all our families would spend together.

The memories of that summer vacation are still vivid in my mind. Getting sick on eating too much ice cream was awesome. Reaching the top 3 scores on the arcade games was awesome (at least until the games were unplugged). Watching my crazy goofball brothers and cousins flying naked into the lake was awesome. Watching my sisters beat the crap out of the Douche bag brothers was even more awesome. The entire experience was incredible, and looking back many years later, aside from meeting my wife and the birth of my children, that summer vacation was one of the greatest experiences of my life.

For the summer vacation of 1982, we were surrounded by our Aunts and Uncles and cousins and I also had my best friend with me. How do you put into words the emotional roller coaster experience we shared during those six weeks? Me and James grew up together, went off to college together and would be the best man at each other's wedding. We stayed in touch with Johnny and Sonya as often as we could and we still tried to get together whenever we were near each other.

One night many years later when Johnny was in town, the three of us went to Bob's Bar to drink some beer and play pool. We're watching the games, talking about sports and for some reason we started talking about the summer of 1982. Then a tidal wave of memories overwhelmed us. We laughed at everything that happened from the goofballs crashing into the lake, James at the swimming pool and the douche bags getting slammed in the face with cake. And of course talked about our big sisters and how they made our summer vacation awesome, in more ways than we could imagine.

We continued to reminisce about those magical six weeks. But as James is getting ready to shoot the ball he pauses…drops his stick to his side and looks up at me and Johnny and says, "Hey remember the Angels?"

Wow…the Angels. Haven't heard that name in over 30 years.

For the rest of the night, we continued to talk about the girls we called Charlie's Angels. We all instantly remembered the names and looks of Jacklyn, Kate and Farrah. We joked about the first time we saw them at the arcade with drool dripping down our chins, well me and James'. The crazy crash that Johnny had into the creek. The time at the restaurant when me and James spilt ice cream all over our hands and then ran away like little girls. We talked about all the walks, bike rides, zip lining, swimming and canoeing. We talked about the first time we actually spoke to them on the docks and then as if we got bonked on the head, we finally realized why our big sisters wanted to spend that day with us.

Then we started to talk about the last sunset. At first, me and James joked with Johnny because he didn't know how to kiss, even though he was the first one to do so. But then as guys being guys,

James and Johnny teased me for being too afraid to make the move. We talked about Jacklyn, Kate and Farrah and wondered how their lives turned out. Where do they live now? Are they still friends? Are they married and have kids? But in this particular moment we wonder have they ever thought about the summer of 1982?

The memories and stories just rushed out. The more we talked about them the more it seemed like we were put in a time capsule to the very first day we saw them. Then for some reason Johnny asks if we remember the last wave. I'm not sure why he felt he needed to bring that up but then something inside of us just happened. How could we not remember?

We all stopped talking and instinctually look up as if chasing down those memories. Nothing really needed to be said or could be said. The three of us are forever connected because of the life experience we shared that cherished summer. We then look down and just stare at each other with the reflection of a beautiful moment together. I guess the memory was just too pure of our longest walk from their front porch because all three of us had that painful heart wrenching look. It's as if we went back in time and can still see the girls standing on the porch, waving to us with tears streaming down their faces.

Here we are three grown men standing in middle of the pool room at Bob's Bar and just like when we were 13, we turn towards each other and share the biggest hug with tears in our eyes. Only this time, unfortunately we didn't have our big sisters to hold us and tell us it would be ok. But in this moment we finally understood why our big sisters were waiting for us with their arms wide open ready to help heal our hearts. We met our first girlfriend and had our first kiss. We had our first love and ultimately experienced our first heart break. We spent an entire lifetime of emotions of laughter, joy, tears and sorrow in a short span of just six weeks.

It's amazing how after so many years go by and if you allow yourself, you can go back in time and have the exact same emotions and feelings you had at that moment. You can remember the sweaty palms the first time you held hands. The anxiousness you felt about the first kiss. And the incredible sadness of knowing it will all come to an end.

Years later; me, Johnny and James would find the love of our lives, get married and be blessed with beautiful children. But in that one moment, for that night we didn't think about our kid's birthdays, mortgages or jobs. Instead, we were 13 all over again with Charlie's Angels; sitting on the dock watching another sunset, walking under the stars holding hands and then standing on the front porch one last time. The six of us: James and Jacklyn, Johnny and Kate and me and Farrah. The first girls we got enough courage to talk to, our first hand holding experience, our first awkward kiss, our first real girlfriends…our first Angels.

The End…